The Elementals:

The Quest

The Elementals:

The Quest

Sharada M Subrahmanyam

PARTRIDGE
A Penguin Random House Company

ISBN:	Hardcover	978-1-4828-4910-3
	Softcover	978-1-4828-4908-0
	eBook	978-1-4828-4909-7

Print information available on the last page.

To order additional copies of this book, contact
Partridge India
000 800 10062 62
orders.india@partridgepublishing.com

www.partridgepublishing.com/india

1

Antheia

The day started normally. Then again, all life-changing days do.

Hey, I'm Antheia Jeune. This is the detailed report on the Legend of the Fifteen. This is the first time I'm doing something like this; so don't expect me to get everything in standard format. We'll be telling this in different people's points of view. Oh, who are we? You'll see.

The best place to begin, I suppose, is the beginning.

We started out the day pretty much as usual – Arbre Jeune (Not my brother) yelled at me to wake up, and I yelled at everybody else to get up. Then we went to 'develop our own type of magic', as Bianca put it, and then we did the other types of magic. It went pretty good – at least for me. Then we went to grab some food, and I saw my best friends – Máni Mond, Helios Soliel, Karus Kostbare and Astrum Estrella. Ours was an odd group, what with two sets of opposite magic chatting like they'd never fought.

"The moon just reflects the light from the sun!"

"Only if you talk scientifically!"

Strike that. Mostly chatting like they'd never fought.

At lunch, we noticed something odd. The Seven (The seven most powerful Elementals gathered by our leader, Bianca Luminis, to fight the Dark) were huddled together and discussing something very seriously. As I glanced at them, I felt a slight disturbance, like the Balance was getting upset. I shrugged off the feeling and got back to eating. Towards the end of the meal, Stervia got up and came to us, real casually. She whispered, "Meet us in the auditorium in five minutes." Then she left.

Five minutes later, my friends and I stood in the auditorium. The Seven were already there. They seemed to be arguing about something.

"We really mustn't send so many people! Resources are sparse enough!" Pianta Jeune whispered loudly.

"Softly!" Bianca chastened.

"But, Pianta," said Selena Soliel. "The more people we send, the better their chances of success!"

"And the higher the likeliness-"

"Enough." Albus Patronus, Bianca's second in command and close friend, ordered.

"We'll send all five of them. Besides," she added dryly. "If we are attacked, I doubt five people will be able to do much."

"Ella-"

"Cut it out, Stren. They're here." I guess I forgot to mention – Bianca's name used to be Ella Elementa and Albus was Stren Elementa. Their names changed after this war we had recently. They *still* hadn't gotten used to their new names, and it had been almost two months since the war ended. I grinned and waved. "Hey!"

Bianca nodded. "Hi."

"What's going on?" Karus asked.

"In a nutshell, a lot. We're issuing a quest."

I frowned. "Why do we need five people for this one?" I enquired.

"Don't we usually have a quest for a new Elemental?"

"What's so special about this one?"

We kept bombarding them with questions, until Bianca used her favorite spell: "Ruhe!" And we couldn't speak. Very simple, very effective. Under normal circumstances, I would have grinned. This time, however, I scowled. Bianca grinned. She removed the Silence from the rest of the seven, but the rest of us still couldn't speak.

"This is an official quest." Stren. said, as though that explained everything. Máni mouthed, "What?"

Stren glared at Pianta. "All the old campers know, eh?"

Pianta grinned and explained. "It's a traditional quest." My jaw dropped. God, we hadn't had a traditional quest in, like, a hundred years. What could possibly be the matter?

"So," Ella said, shaking me out of my reverie. "Do you accept?" I raised my eyebrows. She smiled sheepishly. "Sorry. Sie können sprechen. Well?"

"What's it about?"

"We will only tell you if you accept. But we can say that the fate of the world depends on the quest." Cielo said.

"Melodramatic, much?" Astrum asked.

"No." Lau said. "*That* is putting it lightly. All life and Light on Earth depends on it." I was stunned. *Life and Light?* God, it must be bad. I glanced at the others and talked via our communication stone (another long story for another time). *Well?*

I don't know. Said Helios. *It must be important.*

No, duh, Sherlock. That was Máni.

I stopped them before they could have another argument. *I say we accept. Máni?*

Yeah. Astrum?

I don't think so. Karus?

I agree with Astrum. Helios?

He hesitated, and then sighed. *I hate to say this, but I think we should accept. I can't believe I am in agreement with Mond.*

I smiled and withdrew from the connection. "We accept." We chorused. "So, what's it about?" I added.

Bianca added some anti-eavesdropping spell, and then started. The more I heard, the more apprehensive I got.

First, she told us about this ancient library. There, Pas Oloi Elementa had guarded the knowledge of the ancients. There was a special set of lenses, which have the power to reveal some deep secrets. They had six pairs, but there were supposed to be 13. The rest of the seven were with Malvagita Ubella and Cattiva Mauvaise (The two evil guys they defeated during the war). Now that they were dead, the lenses location was not known by most (At this point, I felt like saying, 'of course not, most don't even know of their existence'). This would not be a problem, except Malvagita had summoned this huge army of shades, who would attack in five days, at sunset. Then she told us how those two came together. The scrolls contained some knowledge, but the most important knowledge was the spells that were contained in a scroll about Prima Lingua. Bianca had read as much as she could, but there was so much more to that knowledge. I understood why they were so desperate. They had no idea about the size of the army, or if they contained any Anima Tueurs (Soul slayers). Though Bianca had stayed here only for three months, and Albus for even less time, they still felt this place was home. I knew how they felt. I set my jaw and asked, "Do you have any idea where we should start?"

Bianca glanced at Albus, and they unconsciously stepped closer to each other. Bianca waved her hand and summoned an image. "We Saw some stuff. Had some visions. That's how we know about the army. We saw some of the locations, some three places. And – well, it's not good news, to say the least."

I glanced at the screen that Bianca had summoned, and my mood soured even more. The first location was some kind of desert – cold kind. It faded really quickly. Another was some kind of mountain, really tall. The third location was easy to recognize – the sphinx. I looked at Bianca and Albus. "The bad news?" I asked. Bianca scowled.

"The first is Aurora Borealis. The second is Mount Everest, Himalayas, Nepal. Tallest peak in the world. The third is the Great Sphinx of Giza. The thing is – you need to find the other places yourself. The Darkness should be both a hindrance as well as a blessing – They are all protected by shades and other Dark magic, so it should be easier to locate, but hard to get past. There are eight such locations." She hesitated, shifting ever so slightly. "There is another thing you should know."

Albus took it from there. "They need to be taken in a certain order – The first with the most protection and the last with the least." I scowled. They just had to make it more difficult, didn't they? "You need to be able to detect and differentiate magic really well, able to adapt to changing conditions. You guys are the most suited for this." He took a deep breath. "Apart from that-"

"There's more?" I demanded, frowning.

Albus nodded. "You also need to get back in eight days, at most. You need to get back and join the fight."

I glanced at my friends, and their jaws were set like they were ready for anything. I turned back to Bianca. "We'll leave as soon as we pack." Then, we stalked out, leaving the Seven staring at us, dumbfounded.

II

Antheia

I finished packing, and got to a quiet place so we could leave quickly. The others were already there waiting for me. We got ready to leave, but the Seven appeared. I guessed they did a Find, and a moment later, Pianta confirmed it. "Told you I got it right." She told Cielo. The latter just rolled her eyes and turned to us.

"We need to tell the rest of the campers about the quest." She said abruptly. I frowned.

"Won't that cause a lot of panic?" I asked.

"Yes, but it is necessary." Albus said.

"Why?" Astrum asked.

Albus glanced at Bianca. She took a deep breath and said, "I have the gift of prophecy, the gift of Manteía." She ignored our incredulous expressions and continued. "I spouted a prophecy yesterday.

> *The world's fate is intertwined*
> *With the fate of the quest of five*
> *They shall go to the corners of the world*
> *And five shall survive*
> *The people shall be told of their next fight*
> *A hidden enemy shall be unveiled at night*

> *And the fate of the friendship so bright*
> *Shall be decided by a choice by the Light.*

"So I decided that we need to send five people on the quest." By the time Bianca finished, our mouths were hanging open wide.

"Close your mouths, people," said Lau.

"Or a fly might get in." Selena finished.

We snapped our mouths shut. Helios pursed his lips. "Why don't you tell the people after we've gone?"

Stervia shook her head. "Tradition."

"Let's go," said Albus. We teleported to the Auditorium. Everybody was already there. Suddenly, there was a bright flash of light. When the glow lessened, we could see the figure of a girl. This probably sounds rather childish or naïve, but it looked like an angel.

She spoke.

"They know the situation now, Sister." Bianca gasped.

"Isabella?" She whispered, eyes wide. "But – but you left us! Disappeared!"

The glow faded completely. Isabella flew to Bianca, who took a step back. "Yes," Isabella said, her voice heavy. "I left. I came here, and was introduced as Kate." I gasped, my eyes wide. Kate – Katharine – she'd been dead for a year now! "I was always…different. My amulet tied itself around my neck. After a few months, I got a dream. I didn't understand it, but when I woke up, I was like this." She raised her arms and stretched her wings. "I learnt that I was to help protect the Elementals. The Amulet – Well, I have a burn now." She paused, and said, "I'm sorry, Ella."

Bianca's eyes softened, and she said, "You needn't apologize, Bella."

Kate – Isabella – whoever she was – smiled. Then she said, "On a completely different note, I can tell you the location of the first two places. Questers, please step forward." The five of us stepped forward. "Listen carefully. The first one is in the Coliseum, in Rome. You will go there immediately. The second is in Mount Everest." Then she turned towards Bianca one last time, and smiled. "Later, Bianca Luminis." She disappeared, and I scowled. I thought she'd give us two more locations, not one! I sighed internally, and shouldered my bag. The rest of the five did the same. "When are we leaving, Bianca? We don't have much time."

Bianca nodded. "Summon the wall and say, Rome. It's the quickest way to move across worlds." Camp was in a parallel world, with the time running similarly to the other. I nodded, and left the auditorium. Astrum summoned the wall, and stepped through. The rest of us followed suit.

As soon as I got there, I realized I had a very sparse knowledge of Latin.

This was going to be a long week.

I scowled slightly as I tried to interpret the directions a Roman was trying to give us. Finally, he grunted and gestured for us to follow him. I tried not to scowl harder as we followed the man. We'd lost three hours already, trying to get to the Colosseum. During a quest with time so limited, three hours was costly. However we finally got there.

"Wow." I stared at in awe. The place was amazing, except-

I closed my eyes, and took a deep, calming breath. There was so much Darkness in the place. We needed to get out of there, and get out of there fast. Did I mention get out of there?

We walked to the queue and got five tickets. The man at the counter said something irritably in Latin. I didn't need an interpreter to know he was asking for money. Máni pulled out her wallet and got a wad of euros. "Um, Quanto?" She said referring to a dictionary she had in one hand.

The guy told his rate and we went through. As soon as we were out of earshot of the mortals, I demanded, "How did you do that?"

Máni smirked. "Unlike some people, I come prepared." I glared at her. Her smile just widened, but she explained. "I put a spell on this to make it look neat, and stuffed some money in here. I just dump it in there, and pull it out whenever I need it." I nodded, though I still had more questions. There were matters more pressing than the wallet.

We walked with the tour crowd, keeping an eye out for any possible hiding place. The tour guide went on and on and on, but I didn't pay attention. Suddenly, I felt a prickling at the base of my neck, and turned. There was nothing there, but the shadows were behaving strangely, like they were trying to pull us. I told the others using my MindSpeech, and walked on. Suddenly, Helios stiffened. I glanced at him, and he mouthed, *Slip away.* I nodded, and alerted the others. We waited a moment, and then walked to the side quietly. As soon as we were out of the group's sight, I felt a pressure building up on my MindBarriers. I tensed, and readied myself for a fight.

Not a moment too soon.

My barriers broke, and I felt great Darkness. I staggered, and shouted in my mind, *Stereá kai adýnami!* I screamed a reveal spell.

The darkness solidified into a single form, and I nearly screamed. The Darkness had transformed into a…

…A basilisk.

The winged creature roared, and I froze. *Not real.* I kept telling myself that. *Just an illusion.* I took a deep breath, and drew my

MindSword. It glowed with the Light, and the basilisk briefly faltered. I attacked in that moment, dodging venom and slashing at its wings. I racked my brain as I tried to remember how to defeat it. It was some kind of small animal...*Duck! Roll! Try cutting off its wings!* I remembered all the training lessons.

I recalled what Bianca had taught us during our lessons. *The Basilisk reputed to be king of serpents and said to have the power to cause death with a single glance. Its weakness is in the odor of the weasel.* Bianca had been reading from a book, and had looked up. *Actually, its not the odor of the weasel but the weasel itself. They are natural enemies.*

I felt some pain on my arm, and scowled. I slashed with my MindSword and summoned a weasel. Enough said.

The basilisk retreated, and I opened my eyes. I realized that I was on the ground and tried to get up. I felt nauseous immediately. I eased back down and tried again. This time I was able to sit up. I glanced to my right, and saw that the others were lying down with their eyes closed too. I looked away, and saw a security guard walking towards us. I quickly cast a invisibility spell over us and closed my eyes. The spell had taken too much energy. Next to me, Astrum groaned and got up. I told him to be silent, and he nodded. Then he glanced at my arm, and his eyes widened. I glanced down too, and bit back a yell. The basilisk had cut my hand, and the wound was poisoned.

III

Astrum

I glanced at Antheia's arm, internally screaming. How in the worlds had she managed to get *that*? I shook my head. Time for questions later. I extended my hand and indicated that she should do the same. She tried and winced. I scooted closer and gently took her arm myself. I Pulled out some healing Resinæ (Healing Balm), and applied it on her hand. It would slow the poison, but Helios was best at healing poisons. I bandaged the wound the best I could, and Pulled her upright. She glanced to the side, and took a deep breath. "What happened?" She asked softly.

"We were attacked in our minds."

"No, really? I mean, What form did your attack take?"

I gulped. "A... a *Jorōgumo.*"

"What's a Jorōgumo?"

"It's in a Japanese legend. It's has magical powers, can turn into an attractive human, has a strong venom, and has lived for four hundred years, and that's the youngest." Antheia nodded, and I asked, "What about for you?"

She turned pale. "A basilisk." Whoa. Her worst fear is of snakes, and she had to fight the worst of them? And she won, getting away with only a small cut? Impressive.

I glanced at the others, and looked back at Antheia. I told her to stay put, and went to help Helios.

It was bad.

His attack took the form of...

...A werewolf.

His worst fear, and its something as small as a werewolf?

I shook my head, and slashed my sword. I managed to cut off one of its legs, and it howled. I slashed again, and it disintegrated. I withdrew, and Helios opened his eyes.

"Antheia." I said shortly, and went to help the others.

I finished everything and helped the others up, and went to Antheia and Helios. Helios looked worried.

"We need some of the Light's pure form." He said as soon as he saw us.

"How long, Helios?" Antheia interjected. I was impressed by how steady her voice was.

Helios frowned and examined the cut again. "Six days, seven at best."

Antheia nodded, and got up. I was at her side at once, and started taking her good arm. She shook her head slightly, closed her eyes. I glanced at her arms and saw what she was trying to do. I closed my eyes as well and extended my arms. I felt Antheia and Máni touch my fingertips. We merged our minds, and started a spell. It was to locate the source of all the darkness, basically. As soon as we were done with the spell, I opened my eyes. We followed the spell and came in front of the wall. I stared at it, and scowled. I glanced at the others, and they seemed just as frustrated as me. Slowly, Karus opened his eyes wide. He extended his arm, and whispered, "Apokalýpste." I glanced back at the wall, and my eyes widened. Carved into the wall were these runes:

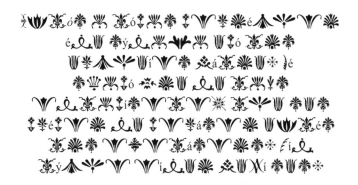

"What runes are these?" I asked out loud.

Karus and Máni looked at each other. "Prima Lingua." They said in unison.

I waited. "Translation?"

They frowned. "The ancient-"

"Not for Prima Lingua, for the runes!" I said, exasperated.

They rolled their eyes. "*Aftós o tópos periéchei éna sýnolo apó tis archaíes mátia. Mé skopó gia na tous entopísete, tha sas prépei na perásei aftés tis exetáseis. Tín týche eínai mazí sas.* Figure out the meaning yourself."

"As gínei étsi." We said. Suddenly, the wall crumbled, and we stood in front of a tunnel.

We had gotten there.

"Will we ever get out of this labyrinth?" Máni said, annoyed.

We had been in the tunnel for hours, and I was beginning to get irritated. Suddenly, Helios stopped.

"What did you call this place?" He asked Máni.

"Um, a labyrinth."

Helios' eyes glinted. "That's it, guys! It's a labyrinth! An ancient maze!"

I turned around. "I don't see how this helps us."

Helios just laughed. "How have you been finding your way around this thing?"

Antheia said what the rest of us were too embarrassed to say. "Guesswork."

"Precisely. Now, what happened to that spell we were using?"

I nearly face palmed. The solution was so simple, like all ancient labyrinths' solutions were. "It must be like the Cretan labyrinth. All that was needed for that was a *really* long string and a good sense of hearing."

Helios rolled his eyes. "All labyrinths are modeled on that one."

I frowned. "But how is a Greek style labyrinth in the middle of Rome?"

"The romans took on certain Greek concepts."

I nodded, and turned. The darkness was greater towards the left. I took a deep breath and walked into the tunnel in the left.

A blast of wind came out, like someone or something had teleported out the 'Dark way'. I went deeper into the tunnel and stepped into a circular room. The others drew weapons and made an arrow-head formation with me at the tip. We walked forward, and I drew my spear. In the middle of the room, there was a pair of blue lenses. I cautiously walked towards them, and reached out. There was a bright flash of light, and the lenses materialized as a bracelet on Antheia's wrist.

We had done it.

IV

Astrum

We all stood stunned for a minute. I decided it was time to get something done.

I took Antheia's arm, and examined the lenses. It was nothing special, just a clear blue piece of glass. What really caught my eye was the perfect shape. I slowly averted my eyes, and Antheia yanked her arm back. She opened her pack, and took a sip of *dýnami*, and passed the bottle around. I took a sip, and felt energized immediately. We glanced at each other, and Antheia took a look at the lenses, and gasped. Helios was at her side in an instant.

"Venenum revelare." There was a short glow, and Helios frowned. "There's less venom in here. How is that even possible?"

Antheia took a deep breath. "I don't know anything about that, but I Saw something in there. Have a piece of paper and a pen?" Máni gave her one, and she drew something on it. "Here, take a look. I think its Prima Lingua."

"Its prima lingua script, but English words. 'Travel next to Mount Everest, young ones. I shall see you there. Do not disappoint me. –Isabella.' Nice handwriting, by the way." Karus said.

There was a pause. "A trap?" I asked.

Helios shook his head. "She told us that earlier today, remember? She became a Veritas vates. They can't lie."

The rest of us nodded. I summoned a set of hiking clothes for everyone, and summoned the wall. "Mount Everest."

We stepped through the wall and arrived at a peak. I looked around, and gasped. It was so beautiful.

Suddenly, I heard a squeak, and whirled around. I stood face to face with Karus. He was so pale, and his eyes were closed tightly. I grasped his arm, and whispered, "Open your eyes, Karus." He didn't respond. "Kostbare." Still nothing. "Stone."

"I told you not to call me that." He said weakly.

"*I* told you to open your eyes. Did you listen?"

"I'm acrophobic." He said. I rolled my eyes.

"Really? I never could have guessed." I said sarcastically. "I'm arachnophobic."

He peeked out. "Seriously?"

I nodded. "Yup."

We cautiously turned, and I saw the others step out of the wall. Helios was last. He stiffened as soon as he got out, and scrambled down the slope as soon as he could.

"Wait!" I yelled. "Helios!" Karus and I began getting down, Karus seemingly forgetting all about his acrophobia. I heard the others climb down as well.

We didn't get very far.

As we raced down, the ice suddenly gave away, and we fell into a small chamber. I got up and drew my sword. This place was obviously Dark.

"Take your spear." Karus whispered.

I grabbed the spear and then sheathed my sword. I stepped forward a bit and heard a low growl. The others came up too, and we stood back to back, at least, as much as we could with four people in the set. I glanced to the side and saw a pair of yellow eyes staring at me. I pointed my spear at it and whispered, "Lámpoun." My spear tip glowed, and I waved it about. I saw three wolves, and I heard the others gasp as well. I guessed they'd seen some too them too.

Wolves…these were no wolves. Their eyes looked almost human. They were werewolves.

I gripped my spear harder, and glared at the werewolves. One of them crept forward towards Antheia, thinking her to be the weak link.

It was wrong.

Antheia swung her spear, shouting, "Elementa!" The werewolf got a good-sized cut on its side, and yelped. It turned and went behind another werewolf.

The one in front of me transformed. "Hello, Astrum Estrella, Antheia Jeune, Máni Mond, Karus Kostbare. Welcome to my humble home. But where is Helios Soliel?" His lip curled in disgust as he said Soliel, but he covered it within a fraction of a second. I wondered if I had imagined it.

"He isn't here." Karus answered.

"I noticed." The man sniffed the air. "He is somewhere near. I can sense him. Find Venato!" He directed the last part to the wolf behind him. It scrambled off, and returned a moment later with another wolf. "Venato, get Helios." I studied the man in the mean time.

He was well built, if a little dirty, and wore around his neck a strung claw. I looked at his face, and found certain similarities between him and someone I know. He looked a lot like…

"Helios." I said. "You're Helios' father."

He bared his teeth in a smile. "Yes." He said, amused. "Daniel Wolf. Nice to meet you!"

Karus scowled. "Wish we could say the same."

Way to be polite and rude at the same time.

"Now, if you guys don't mind, put your spears away. It's rude." Wolf added.

"No way." I retorted. "You're a creature of the dark."

He snorted. "A creature of dark, you say." The other wolf, Venato, returned with another wolf that was pure white. "What's this, then, a white werewolf?"

The Werewolf growled at Daniel, but the latter transformed and growled right back. The white one tensed, and Daniel snapped at it. The white wolf dodged and stopped in front of us. It bared his teeth, and I glanced at its fur. On the white, standing out in golden, was the mark of the Sun.

V

Karus

"Helios," Antheia whispered. I glanced back at the white wolf, and saw the mark of the Sun on its back.

The wolf transformed into Helios. He drew his spear. "Hello, Father." He spat.

Daniel smiled. "Lupus, my child. How are you?"

"Better off without you." He retorted.

Daniel laughed. "Still no sense of humor?"

"Plenty," Helios said. "I just don't think this situation called for any humor."

"True enough." Daniel sighed. "Let's get straight to the point, shall we? Rejoin our pack, Lupus."

Helios scowled. "Never."

The wolves started growling, but Daniel snapped at them (not literally). They stopped growling, but they stared at us. I did my best to stare them down, but I got the feeling that they weren't going to tolerate another refusal.

"Consider carefully. You-"

"I've already considered, thanks. Now, give us the lenses." How direct.

Daniel didn't answer. Instead, he transformed, and growled. Six wolves attacked, but Antheia yelled, "Elementis Vindico!" The wolves were blasted away, and Helios transformed. I tentatively tried to merge my mind with his, and it worked. I relaxed and told the others to do the same thing with my communication stone. They did that, and gripped their spears.

I shall form my own pack, Alpha. I heard Helios was saying.

Daniel bared his teeth. *The laws of the pack require you to have another companion before you leave it. A female wolf.*

Helios growled. *It seems that you have changed the laws since I left.*

The pack as a whole did the changing.

There are no females in our pack.

Then you cannot leave.

Yes he can. I jumped. It was Máni.

Silence, Human.

No, you shut up. She turned to Helios. *I offer.*

There was a sudden silence, and Daniel bared his teeth again.

No way, Mond. You've got no idea what you're offering to do.

Shut up, Soliel.

Yes, Lupus. Be silent. Venato, do it.

NO! Helios roared, and snapped at Venato, baring his teeth.

Alpha? Venato asked.

He smiled. *Let Lupus do it.*

She's actually going to do it, I thought. *Máni's going to become a werewolf.*

She knelt in front of Helios, and extended her arm. Helios turned away, but Daniel growled. *Now, Lupus.*

Helios looked at us in despair. *I'm sorry, Máni.* He slowly reached forward, and nipped her lightly in the arm.

She screamed.

Helios crouched and snarled. The rest of the wolves backed away. A moment later, Máni transformed.

I watched in both horror and fascination as Máni became a wolf.

She was a silvery wolf, with blue eyes, like her human self. I glanced at Helios' eyes, which were golden, again like his human self.

Slowly, Máni got up, and the wolves went further back and bowed. *Lupa,* they said, and gathered behind Helios. *We shall join their pack, Alpha.*

Daniel growled. *Be gone with you!*

Helios bared his teeth. *No, Próta. You shall leave.* He roared (do wolves roar?) and Daniel backed away. Helios growled, and Máni attacked.

She bit Daniel on the leg, and he howled and burst into a bright light. I covered my eyes, and when I opened them again, Daniel was gone.

Helios and Máni transformed back into humans, and Helios told one of the wolves to get some water. They washed their mouths, and drank some of it. Suddenly, Antheia collapsed, and Helios was at her side in an instant. "Stamatíste!" He yelled, and she took a deep, shuddering breath.

"Thanks."

"You're welcome." He turned to the rest of the wolves. "This is a white pack. So, right now, my friends and I will do a purifying spell to drive the Dark out. OK?"

The wolves growled, and they must have meant yes, since Helios said, "Three, two, one. Katharíste!" We said the last part together. There was a sudden shift, and the wolves' skin shimmered. They became either grey or brown. Helios smiled. "Stay out of sight, but in hearing range." They ran off.

"Does that include me as well, Alpha?" Máni asked teasingly.

"No, but maybe I could tell you to shut up, since I'm your Alpha." Máni groaned. "Please don't."

Helios smiled. "Your wish is granted, Lupa. So, guys, Let's go get the lenses?"

"No need." A miffed voice said. "I've already done it." Isabella came into sight. "I just came to tell you that you can use the lenses to find the next location, but I suggest you stay here for some time, like, overnight. You've found two pairs, and you really need some rest. Here you go." She extended her hand, and a pair of green lenses floated towards Máni. "Bye."

And she disappeared, leaving us staring dumbfounded at the place where she disappeared.

VI

Karus

I blinked, and turned to Máni. Helios was next to her (again), and Máni was holding the lenses. She was staring at them in a trance, and Helios was looking at her, but not seeing her. I started moving towards the duo, but Helios suddenly looked up and snapped, "Stop!" I froze. He took a deep breath. "She's Seeing the next place."

"Why-"

"Later." He stared at the lenses now. A moment later, Máni looked up.

"I give you three guesses." She grinned.

There was a pause. "Egypt." I said.

"Wrong."

"Kalahari." That was Astrum.

"Nope." Helios replied.

Antheia frowned. "Parthenon. Greece." She said decisively.

"Right." The girls shared a grin.

The rest of us stared at Antheia in disbelief, and she shrugged. "The first was Roman. So I figured this one must be Greek, to keep some variety. Famous place in Greece – Parthenon."

I shook my head. Helios smiled. "You'd be a great addition to the pack. Want to join?"

"You kidding, right?" Antheia asked warily. Helios shook his head, and Antheia narrowed her eyes. "No thanks. I'll pass." Helios looked disappointed, but nodded.

"So, who's setting up camp?" I asked, more to break the silence than anything else.

Antheia threw a bead at me, but I moved a little. Knowing her, it was probably designed to expand once it hit something.

I was right.

As soon as it hit the ground, it expanded, and transformed into a tent. "Cool!" Astrum yelled, and dove right onto the tent. I followed suit. I vaguely heard Antheia say, "Boys."

"I agree." Máni said, entering the tent. She wrinkled her nose, and withdrew. "I'll sleep out, guys."

"I'll keep first watch." Helios said.

There was a sudden noise outside, and went out of the tent. Antheia had thrown another bead, and had slapped a third into her bracelet.

"What're you staring at?"

"Nothing, Ant."

A vine suddenly grew and lifted me upside-down. High. "Don't even think about calling me that again, Rock. Clear?" Antheia warned, glaring at me with a ferocity that, though well known, was still seriously scary. I mean, you-haven't-been-scared-till-you've-seen-it scary.

I gulped and nodded. She let me down, and I moved to the tent.

Helios and Máni transformed outside the tents, and took their positions – Máni certainly didn't look like she was sleeping.

I shook my head. God knows why she volunteered, 'cause I sure don't.

VII

Helios

As I transformed, I saw Karus glance at us and shake his head. He was probably thinking, *werewolves. What next?*

I saw Antheia sitting next to Máni, and I turned away. I don't know what I was thinking when I offered. Being an Elemental was tough enough, especially now, but being a werewolf and an Elemental was supremely difficult. And now, Máni was one too, when she didn't have to.

I don't know what Máni was thinking when she volunteered to become a werewolf. Then she became Lupa. So ours became the most powerful pack.

See, ages ago, the wolves had captured a seer, who managed to buy her way out by giving three small predictions that was related to the werewolves. One, there would come a White werewolf into the pack. Two, all the wolves, except for the White one, would be enlisted to help a Dark Elemental. Three, a silver werewolf, Lupa, would be created, and whichever pack she was a part of would become the most powerful pack. So, when Máni joined my pack as Lupa, my pack became powerful. The other wolves joined my pack because of that – survival instincts. But maybe – just maybe – our pack became powerful because the other wolves joined it.

I was interrupted in my musings when another wolf, Legatum, came up to me. *Some thing is approaching.*

What is it?

We are not sure. It seems to be a small thing, but it has destroyed an entire camp of humans down the slope.

What does it look like?

Like a human. It smells like something else, though.

Like what?

A little sweet, a little sour, a little bitter. It's impossible to describe.

I nodded. *Máni, go check it out.*

Máni darted out, a silver blur in the darkness. She returned a second later. She relayed her memories to me, and I got up. Antheia got up, but I shook my head. If she got into any more action, the poison would spread faster. *Get the boys will you, Legatum? I'll go and see this thing for myself.*

Yes, Alpha.

I got out, and immediately, a smell reached me. I froze and wrinkled my nose. It smelled like a sweet would smell if it were dipped in lime-juice and bitter gourd. But at the same time, it wasn't disgusting. It was more... inviting. I transformed into my Human Form, and nodded at Astrum, who had come out. "Well?" He asked.

"We're not sure. It smells like, sweet, but sour and bitter."

"Sweet but sour and bitter." He repeated, suddenly afraid.

"Yeah, why?" I asked, shooting him a glance.

He ignored me and started climbing down. Suddenly, he froze. "Jorōgumo." He whispered, and started backing up.

I saw a girl was climbing up – long black hair, pale skin, beady black eyes, soft inviting smile – everything that absolutely screamed 'safe'. I drew my sword. A kid climbing up this high – if that's not suspicious, then I don't know what is.

"Hello, Lupus." she said after reaching the little platform outside our cave.

"The name's Helios, not Lupus. You are?"

She smiled. "Arachna."

"What do you want?" Astrum demanded.

Her smile widened. "Some food would be great, but if not – well, I'll settle for a set of five Elementals." She started changing. She was shrinking, and some sharp pincers grew out of her mouth. She grew more legs and eyes. She became a Spider.

I transformed, and howled. Antheia came out, and winked at me. "Thought you might need some help." I snapped at her, and she grinned. She shot some white mist at Arachna, who scuttled away. "All healed," she said, and drew her spear.

I shook my head and stood to her left. *Arrow!* I told the other wolves, and nudged Máni to Antheia's left. Antheia shook her head. "Five in a rank." She told me, and I relayed the order. "Helios, Máni, Transform, if you don't mind. It's easier for the rest of us to cover for you." I nodded and transformed. "Spears out. Swords loose. Now!" She yelled.

"Elementis!" All the girls yelled. I nodded at the Karus, and yelled the same spell, while Karus yelled, "Elementa!" His sword glowed really bright, and he shouted, "Vade!"

Some of the brightness shot towards Arachna, and she stumbled. The rest of us took the opportunity and attacked.

I'd like to say we managed to finish the fight in a moment. The truth? Arachna had other tricks up her sleeve.

A force field erupted around the spider, and we all were thrown down. Before I could get down, some bits of black mist came and held me down. I resisted the hold, but I couldn't even get up an inch. "Let us go!" I yelled.

"Is that what you want, Lupus?" She whispered. I didn't answer. She shot more bits of black mist, but not at me. It went towards Antheia, and went right into her. Her eyes turned pure black, and she got up. Almost every body else was getting up, except for Máni. Their eyes were black, with no whites. They went and stood in the shadows, and slowly started disintegrating.

"NO!" I yelled, and transformed. The shadows couldn't hold me any longer. I leapt up and pushed Antheia out of the shadows, trying to get to the others as well.

The spell broken, the other five tried to fight the Jorōgumo, but she was gone.

The shadows didn't release me, though, and slowly pulled me away, until all at once, I wasn't in the mountain anymore.

Was I underwater? It felt like it, but I could breath. I could feel myself almost floating, but something – chains – was holding me down. I kicked out, trying to see where I was. I was surrounded by darkness, but I could vaguely see a bubble around me, and – was that a throne? Who was that on it? I blinked, trying to adjust to the dark light.

"Isabella?"

VIII

Helios

I stared at her, stunned. "But you're Kate – Katharine! A white Elemental! And you're Ella's sister! How could you? How could you betray us?"

A flicker of impatience came on her face, and she pursed her lips. "Yes, I am Isabella, Ella's sister. No, I did not betray you. Look closer, Soliel. Use your head."

I looked, and saw that she was tied down by mist. I glanced up to her neck and saw an amulet. "But – but how? You said you don't have an amulet anymore. You said-"

"That wasn't me! That was someone else! Or something else, but that's not the point. I was captured, as you must be able to see. Someone or something else seems to have taken my place there. How long have I been missing?"

I thought for a moment. "A year. We thought you died."

Isabella nodded. "I was correct. I have been here for two years."

"How do you know? You would have had a hard time distinguishing between night and day." I said, gesturing, or at least trying to, at the darkness around us.

She shook back her sleeve a little. "A watch. Duh."

I shook my head. "Of course. A watch. How stupid of me."

"Was that sarcasm?" She demanded. I just shook my head and grinned.

Suddenly, I felt someone brush against my mind. *Helios!*

Astrum? I asked tentatively.

Yeah. We managed to get rid of the Jorōgumo, but we dunno where you are. I-

How are Antheia and Máni and Karus?

They're fine. As I was saying, I need to tell the werewolves something.

I thought about it. *The truth.* I said, finally. *Tell them that I have been captured. What happened?*

We're not sure. It was like we were asleep or something. We don't remember much. We just remember being in the cave in the middle of the day, and seeing Arachna. I got my sword out and attacked. The others followed, and we managed to finish her off.

Did you make sure there was no more residual venom in Antheia's blood?

Yes. We used Venenum revelare. No venom. Where are you?

Under-

I felt a slight pressure on my mind barriers. A moment later, the barriers gave way, and some Darkness rushed in. I fought it, but it filled my mind, and I soon lost control. I felt a slight shift, and I soon saw and felt nothing but a soft and warm darkness. I relaxed, and a soft voice urged me, *Lie down.*

But I'm not tired. I tried protesting.

No, you are very tired. You will drop down and float in the water.

I started fighting – what? There was nothing – just some soft comfort. All of a sudden, I felt sleepy. *I will lie down and float in the water.* I agreed.

Good. The voice said. I felt strangely pleased. For some reason, I wanted to make this voice happy. *Now, remove your amulet.*

What amulet? I questioned.

The one on your right hand. It answered. *Remove it and let it float about in the water. What is it to you? It is worthless. A little piece of trash.*

Worthless piece of trash. I agreed. I moved my left hand towards my right and started untying the amulet.

"Helios!" A voice cried, distant. "Helios, stop! Fight it!"

Fight what? I thought. *The warmth?*

"Helios, please! Fight! Fight the Darkness!" The distant voice urged, panicked.

The darkness? The word triggered a memory in me. *Darkness...I am supposed to fight the Darkness.* Memories rushed back into me. I was furious that I was tricked so easily. *I am Helios Soliel, white Elemental. I shall not give in!* (Needlessly dramatic? Ah, well. Never mind. It did work.) I burst out of the darkness and tightened my amulet, but before I could complete it, some dark mist came and moved my hands away. The Amulet could not be removed, but it was loosened. I could loose my source of power.

I could loose my only connection to the rest of the Elemental world.

Bianca and Albus had put some spells on everybody's amulet, so that if the Amulet was not within one and a half meters of an Elemental related thing, then the other Elemental related thing would also not work. They did it to ensure none of the amulet related things would work if it was stolen or misplaced.

I tried to tighten the Amulet with only one hand, but it only got a little looser. I stopped, and tried to get upright. I couldn't. I glanced down, and saw that I was tied to the sea floor with some more black chains. I glanced at Isabella, and saw that she was similarly restrained, except that she was on the throne sort of thing.

"Well?" She asked, glaring at me.

"Thank you." I told her. "Any ideas as to how to get out of this little situation?"

She shook her head. Suddenly, four people swam in. No, wait – they flew in with their wings. Odd. They snapped their fingers, and the chains around me and Isabella shifted a little, so we were no longer tied to the sea bed, but to long Dark Lámpsi ánthi boards. We floated a little away, and passed a little shield sort of thing. We moved into a little chamber sort of thing. There were two people in a heated discussion. Next to them was a board with a mini version of – it was Camp!

I turned my attention to the two people in front. They turned towards us, and I gasped.

"You!" I yelled.

"Us." One of them agreed. "Nice to see you again, Helios Soliel. We've been waiting for you."

IX

Máni

I paced in front of Astrum as he tried to contact Helios through the communication stone. Helios behaved like a fool, pushing away Antheia like that. He just disappeared, and I had to get everyone awake. They didn't even realize that they had been under an enchantment, and when they woke up, they finished off Arachna. She just dissolved into black mist, so I don't think she's dead.

I turned and saw Astrum open his eyes. "Well?" I demanded.

"He said that he was captured, and we had to tell the werewolves that. He also wanted to know what happened, and how the rest of you were."

"Did he say anything else about the pack?"

"Nope."

I nearly yelled in frustration, and transformed back into wolf. I tried contacting Helios through MindTouch (Werewolves have their own brand of MindTouch), but with no luck. I ran out of the cave and howled, making the rest of the wolves run up to me. *Lupa?*

Dark forces have captured the Alpha. I said, simple and straightforward.

How could dark forces have captured him? Isn't he dark?

I glared at the wolf who had said that (Quite effectively). *This is a* white *pack. Darkness is opposite, so to speak.*

The wolf shrank back. I tilted my head. *Come forward, Skoteinó.* I ordered.

The wolf stepped forward. I transformed, and said, "Katharíste!" A mark appeared on the wolf's back. I stepped forward and looked at it.

I froze.

It was the mark of the dead – the mark of Mors.

I took a step back and said, "Transform, Skoteinó."

He bared his teeth. I took it as, *you don not order us.*

I pursed my lips and tried contacting Helios again. This time, it worked. *Well, Speak of the devil.* I heard Helios think.

I heard that! I said.

Hello, Máni. Can't do this for long. What do you need?

Who's going to lead the pack? Announce it to the rest of the pack.

Lupa will take over. He thought out loud (is that even possible? I don't know.)

Thanks. How are you?

Not good. But I- He cut off, and said, *Got to go.* The connection came to an end.

"So, Skoteinó, transform." He growled, but obeyed.

"What do you want?" He demanded.

"What're you doing with the Mark of Mors?"

"Mark of Morse? I've got Morse code written on my fur?" He laughed nervously. The rest of the wolves started to growl, and he stopped laughing abruptly. "What is your problem?"

"My problem is that you have the Mark of Mors, which is a dark thing, and me and my friends did a cleansing spell strong enough to get rid of it. I did it again now, and I was able to see the mark, indicating that you have some dark thing to hide the mark. So, you either joined the pack late, or you hid the mark with a *lot* of Dark magic."

"Whoa, wolf, breath." He joked. The wolves growled a little more. I raised my hand to stop them.

"Answer me, Skoteinó." I ordered.

He hesitated, and I transformed. I snarled at him and he answered. "I hid the mark with Magic. I'm an Elemental."

A Dark Elemental.

"True. But-"

This is a White pack, Skoteinó.

"Again, true. But I can't help it." I transformed (yes, again. So?) and raised my eyebrows. "Explain. You have one minute."

"I was a White Elemental, gems. Then I got bitten, but it's worse that you think. The Wolf actually managed to bite my amulet as well, so it became Dark. I wasn't a dark Elemental to begin with, so when I transform it became the Mark of Mors. I put a spell on it so that it appears as the Mark of Mors anyway, but I made sure it isn't in clear sight."

I blinked, and said, "Apoteleí af̱tí i ali̱thiní?" I asked. Is this true?

"Naí," He replied. Yes. I asked in Prima Lingua, and he answered in the same, so there was no chance of concealment, unless he has the gift of arguing well. He couldn't have lied to me anyway, since I was the leader of the pack. Should have thought of that.

"Fine. Katharíste." I said, and tried to get rid of the mark. Immediately, I felt a searing pain on the back of my hand, and I nearly collapsed. "Transform, Lupa!" Someone yelled, and squeezed my arm. It was Skoteinó. "Sanare!" He yelled, and the pain eased. I transformed, and Skoteinó eyed me. *A little late, much, Lupa?*

A little late. I agreed. I added out loud, *Stay hidden and guard the rest of the Elementals. I need to be able to contact you all anytime, so stay within audible range. I don't want to have to transform each time. OK?*

Yes, Lupa. The wolves replied.

I ran back to the cave and transformed. "Hi all." I said, and they jumped. "Relax, it's me, Máni."

They relaxed, and Antheia beckoned me forward. "Sit down. We were just deciding when to leave. This is the place. I managed to find out exactly where this set of lenses were."

"And?" I asked.

She grimaced. "Under the Parthenon. We need to get *under* the stand of the Athena Parthenos."

She was greeted by blank stares. She sighed. "The Athena parthenos was a statue of Athena in the middle of the Parthenon. Legend goes that the romans took it. But we need to get under the stand of the Athena Parthenos, unseen."

"Yeah," I said. "That's the toughest part. Any idea what kind of defenses there are around the place?"

"Mortal or Magical?"

"Both."

"No idea whatsoever." She said cheerfully. "That's what we need to find out."

X

Máni

As Karus summoned the wall, I thought about what Helios said. *Don't interrupt me. I am doing a spell.* What spell? I nearly interrupted. *I found our enemy, or rather, our enemies. Those two, again.* I almost interrupted him again, but I stopped myself. *I do not know where we are. I found Isabella. She does not have wings, has an amulet and the gift of Astrapés.* Then, he cut the connection and went back to what he was doing.

"You coming, Máni?" Antheia asked as she went to the wall.

"Yeah." I walked into the wall with her, and pursed my lips. "We need to contact camp and inform them." I said shortly.

They nodded wordlessly. I waited and then sighed. "I guess I'll do it. Angeliofóros tis Elementals, parakaló mas deíxei Bianca Luminis kai Albus Patronus." Messenger of the Elementals, please show us Bianca Luminis and Albus Patronus.

The air in front of me shimmered and we saw Bianca and Albus training. It was amazing to watch.

Bianca cast all sorts of random spells, like smooth, fall, fly, fast, and so on. Albus countered all of them. Bianca suddenly disappeared and Albus' sword flew out of his hand. "No fair!" Albus cried as Bianca reappeared. "You used a wordless invisibility spell, and you haven't taught me that!"

"Of course it's fair." I snapped, making both of them jump. "You can't expect those two to play fair."

"Point taken." He said.

"So, you know." Bianca said. It wasn't a question, but I nodded.

"Helios contacted us. What did he mean when he said Isabella had no wings, had an amulet and the mark of Astrapés?"

Bianca and Albus exchanged a glance. "The mark of Astrapés is control over lightning, except it is really hard to control, so it's more like power over lightning...but it can't control lightning from any other source...you can still get shocked. How did Isabella get it? Maybe mum gave it to her...but-"

"Ells, you're rambling."

"Don't call me Ells." She said absently.

Stren rolled his eyes. "Don't worry about her. She's just worried and nervous."

"Stren, you'll discourage them! And I'm not nervous, it's just that you're so easy to defeat, and I'm not even going full out on you!"

Albus grinned. "Well, *Luminis*, why don't we go full out on each other, then?"

Bianca narrowed her eyes. "You're on, *Patronus*."

They went towards the arena. "Hey, guys!" I yelled. "How about your little fight later? We were discussing something. You ADHD or something?"

"Borderline." They replied at the same time and grinned. I rolled my eyes.

"Are you going to tell the others about the two of them?" Antheia asked.

Bianca hesitated. "No."

"What!" I said (Yelled).

"Why ever would you do that?" Karus said.

"That would discourage them." Albus said.

"No, it won't. They'll feel that it would be easier to defeat them now that you have fought them and know their 'patterns'." Astrum said in one breath.

"Ah." Bianca said.

"Didn't think of that." Albus added.

"Evidently." I snapped.

"What's put a bee in your bonnet?" Albus asked.

Bianca slapped him on the back of his head. "When's the last time you guys ate?" She asked.

"I hunted a few hours back with the pack." I replied absentmindedly.

Bianca's eyes narrowed. "What pack? Hunted? What are you talking about?" I nearly cursed for my slip.

"Well, it's a long story, and we don't have a lot of time. Maybe later?"

"No. Now." Bianca snarled.

"Now what's put a bee in *your* bonnet?" Albus asked, blissfully oblivious to the tense situation.

"Shut up, Stren." Albus laughed at Bianca's reaction. Bianca scowled and must have done some MindSpeech. Albus widened his eyes, and then glared at me suspiciously. I sighed.

"Helios is a werewolf, but he is a white werewolf. He-"

"White, as in color, or as in light?"

"Both. He wanted to leave the pack he was originally in, but they had formulated a new law. He had to leave with a female. There was no female in the pack, so I offered."

"And what kind are you?" Ella demanded.

"White kind, silver color. I'm called Lupa, and Helios is Lupus."

"That doesn't explain what you meant by pack. Have you been biting a few people?"

"No!" I yelled. "The wolves from the other pack left the original pack and came to ours. And before you ask, we purified them. Well, almost all of them."

"Purified or balanced?" She asked, still hostile. "And what do you mean, almost all of them?"

"Purified. One of them has the mark of Mors. I tried to get rid of it." I shrugged. "It didn't work out."

"Why does he have the mark of Mors?"

"'Cause the werewolf who bit him managed to bite his amulet." Bianca nodded and started cutting the connection. "Wait." I said.

"What?" Albus asked.

"Watch." I transformed and showed them the symbol on my back. I transformed back and said, "I'm still the same person."

Bianca's eyes softened. Albus looked confused. Bianca did some more MindSpeech and managed to explain to Albus what was going on. He really was an idiot sometimes. "By the way," said Astrum. "We've gotten two pairs. We're at Greece. Parthenon."

"Congrats! Awesome! What other places do you know?"

"Aurora and Sphinx. We've been to coliseum and mount Everest so far."

"Great!" Albus yelled. "That is so awesome!"

"Yeah." I checked how much energy I had left on my amulet.

I had very little. Now, that's a surprise.

Note the deep sarcasm.

"Running out of charge. See you!" I said, and cut the link.

I thought about what I said. Such a normal reply – it might have been said in better circumstances if I hadn't gone with Florentia Bluma. She was the Elemental who got me to camp. *Stop thinking like that.* I scolded myself. *It's pessimistic.* I turned to the others. "Ready to get the next set?"

XI

Helios

I stared at the people in front of me.

"But you-you died!" I stammered.

"You honestly didn't think we wouldn't have any back up, did you, Lupus?" He asked.

My mind was reeling. In front of us were Malvagita Ubella and Cattiva Mauvaise, the two Dark Elementals Bianca and Albus killed in the war. I tried reaching out with my mind to one of the five, but almost immediately, I felt a searing pain. I writhed, trying desperately to escape the pain, and Isabella screamed, "Stop it! Stop hurting him!" Suddenly, I felt a small tremor. Isabella raised her voice in panic. "Malvagita, stop it! I can't control it!" The pain increased, and I clamped my mouth tightly to prevent myself from screaming out loud. A bolt of red light shot above me, only just missing me. It went and hit Cattiva, who collapsed. Another went and hit one of the winged men.

"Enough, Pýra!" Malvagita yelled. "Stop it, or I shall hurt him more!"

"I can't!" Isabella wailed. *Pýra?* I thought.

"Now!" Malvagita ordered.

"I don't know how to control it!" Malvagita sent some black mist into my air bubble, and I shrieked in pain. I couldn't help it. It was just so much. "No!" Isabella screamed. I felt a slight shift, and then there was no more of the red bolts. "It has stopped, Ubella." Isabella said, her voice shaking. "Now, please, *stop hurting him*."

Malvagita smiled. "Why don't you promise to serve us first?"

"Never!" She screamed, and some more mist trickled into my bubble. Some went into me, and slowly, I felt a small change take place.

"Give me some time, please." Isabella pleaded.

"Oh, you have time." Malvagita said, amused. "The boy will lose control over his physical abilities first, then over his mind. Oh, it will be slow enough at first. He can still speak. If you give in quick enough, perhaps we shall stop the spell. Other wise…well, let's not get into that. You have exactly six and a half days. Decide fast, or we will have to resort to other means." He paused. "Understood?"

"Perfectly." There was some venom in her voice. I glanced at her. *If looks could kill,* I thought. Cattiva got up, and glared at Isabella. "Pýra, personally, I hope you don't decide within the deadline. I shall enjoy the other means."

Malvagita nodded, and the winged men took us back to the room sort of thing.

"What happened? Why did he call you Pýra?"

"I'm a special Elemental." She pulled back her sleeve and showed me her arm. On it was a long red line, but it was slowly changing to black. "This is a dangerous gift. The gift of Astrapés." I gasped and stared at the mark. It was like a lightning bolt. It was difficult to control, but it was the perfect balance. It was useful, but dangerous. It usually came only to wind Elementals usually, since it was control over lightning. But Isabella was a Fire Elemental. I turned back to her face. "My mother gave it to me. She was a wind Elemental, and she thought it would protect me. See, my Elemental powers developed a little early, and it became dangerous. I stopped spending time with Ella, 'cause

I was scared I might hurt her. Then," she sneered, "Malvagita came for me. My mother became worried, and told me how to get to camp. She wasn't sure I could do without help, so she gave me this gift." She smiled wryly. "It's power was too strong. The amulet was not able to get close, so it went to my neck." She sighed, and closed her eyes. "It's more like a curse now. I can't control it, and Malvagita seems determined to get me under his control." She opened her eyes, and I smiled at her.

"At least you are resisting." I said. (I know, I'm hopeless at encouraging people, but you ought to give me credit for trying).

"Yes, but for how much longer?" She asked. "I couldn't stand it if you got hurt on my account." I kept quiet after that. I wondered if she knew the prophecy. I thought about the fourth line. *Five shall survive.* That was a good thing, except prophecies were often unclear. This prophecy was too clear to be true.

The world's fate is intertwined/With the fate of the quest of five. Clear. Our quest succeeds, world survives. Quest fails, world covered in darkness.

They shall go to the corners of the world/And five shall survive. We would go all over the world and survive.

The people shall be told of their next fight. Clear. Everybody knows about the quest and the upcoming fight.

A hidden enemy shall be unveiled at night. Not too sure about that. "What time is it, Isabella?" I asked.

"'Bout eleven PM."

"Thanks."

So, again, clear. I found out about Malvagita at around eleven.

And the fate of the friendship so bright/Shall be decided by a choice by the Light. I thought about that. That part was practically the most confusing part. In fact, it was the only confusing part.

Then my thoughts turned to the other four. What were they doing? *Sleeping, duh.* I thought about Máni. Who was taking charge of the pack? *Máni. Again, duh.* I thought.

I felt someone trying to MindTouch me. *Well, speak of the devil.* I thought to myself.

I heard that! I heard Máni say. Oops.

I glanced at Isabella, who mouthed, *fast.* I told Máni, *Hello, Máni. Can't do this for long. What do you need?*

She sounded miffed, but she replied. *Who's going to lead the pack? Announce it to the rest of the pack.*

Lupa will take over. I thought to the rest of the pack.

Thanks. How are you? She asked, somewhat gratified.

Not good. But I- I cut off. Something else was brushing against my mind. *Got to go.* I cut the connection, and not a moment too soon. The next moment, Malvagita and Cattiva floated up to us. "Hello, Lupus. Who's Lupa?"

"Shouldn't you know?"

Malvagita frowned slightly, but it soon passed. "She has stronger wards. It's annoying, really." He said.

"Good. Isabella, when we get out, remind me to put strong wards around me. I want to annoy this guy." Isabella smiled but said nothing. "I mean, what could-"

"What could possibly be funnier than annoying a guy who could hurt you without even lifting a finger?" Malvagita asked, smiling. The smile didn't reach his eyes. I tried to shoot a bead from the bracelet Bianca gave all of us, but I couldn't move my left hand. I glanced down, and saw...nothing. It was like my hand had disappeared. Malvagita smiled. "Look." He waved his hand, and an image shot up. I saw a set of wings and a hand. There was black mist at the place where the rest of the body must be, making a humanoid shape, except it had wings. I gulped, realizing that the hand was mine, and Malvagita was going to make me another winged servant of his.

"It won't work, Malvagita." I said.

"And why not?"

"Because I am Lupus, Alpha of the pack. Lupa is in my pack. You cannot hurt me." I tried moving my hand again, and it worked. I took a deep breath, closed my eyes, and began a spell.

It was a complicated spell. I concentrated on what I thought was important. Máni. Yes, the completely opposite type of Elemental is the most important on my list. I was the leader of a pack of werewolves. For once that thought didn't startle me. I accepted it. In fact, it was the first time I accepted the wolf part of me.

I then focused on the words. I made sure the spell would undo the Dark spells done by Malvagita and Cattiva. Of course, the spell that helped us to breath was dark, so I had another component to help us breath. I knew all the winged people Malvagita had created were innocent and had to be protected as well, so I did that. I then placed a general spell to protect all white Elementals. Then, I contacted the rest of the five, Bianca, and Stren. I told them what was going on. Finally, I restored balance in the place.

For the second time in my life, I tried a spell that was both dark and White, with the perfect balance. I felt some more power getting added to the spell, and realized that Isabella was helping me restore balance. As soon as the spell was done, I opened my eyes. I frowned. "Where are those two? Please don't tell me they got away."

Isabella winced. "They did. They just disappeared as soon as you started the spell."

I took a deep breath and told her, "Let's go to the surface."

XII

Helios

It turned out that we were at Australia. The locals didn't take much notice. I wondered why that was. Not that I was complaining. Then I notice we were shrouded in white mist with a small touch of lightning. I glanced at Isabella, and saw that she was straining. I touched her shoulder and said, "Stegnósei." All the water evaporated. I did the same for myself.

"Thanks." She said.

"Want some help?" I asked.

She shook her head. "Too dangerous. Its hard enough to control it now, without someone else having to come too."

I nodded, and went back to thinking. Suddenly, I remembered something. Astrum had told me that they used Venenum revelare to check for poison. Yet she was Poisoned by a basilisk. Basilisk venom doesn't just disappear. So, it must have become dormant. This meant that when it came back, it would be much faster, and much stronger as well. It had been dormant for over twenty-four hours, I guessed, so it would reappear soon. Some kinds of poisons were like that. I told Isabella I was going to check on the others for a bit, and she nodded.

"Just don't bang into a wall or something – I don't think the shield covers that," She said.

I reached out with my mind and located Astrum. *How's Antheia?*

She's fine. He said. I could almost imagine him rolling his eyes. *We checked with Venenum Revelare.*

That spell only looks for parts affected by the venom! The venom must be dormant! Basilisk venom doesn't just disappear! Check again!

With which spell?

I rolled my eyes. *I'll try to come there in a couple of minutes. Where are you?*

Outside the Parthenon.

I'm coming. Just hold on. I cut the connection, and glanced at Isabella. "You up to a small trip to Greece?" I asked her.

She smiled. "Are you?" She retorted.

I scowled. "Where did you say they were again?" Isabella asked.

I ground my teeth in frustration. "*Outside the Parthenon.* Those were his exact words."

She glared at me. "Well, contact one of them again and tell them that we're here!"

"I already explained why we can't. They'll probably kill me before recognizing me."

"Well, be gentle then!"

I glared at her, but before I could make a scathing comment, someone contacted me with the stone.

Helios! Where on earth are you? Do a locate spell and come quick! It's Máni here! Antheia is in trouble!

I cursed and grabbed Isabella's hand. "Na lávei mas gia na Ántheia!" I yelled, and the world turned upsidedown.

I blinked, and it was over. "Sorry, Isabella. Emergency." I tried to take a step forward, but Isabella stopped me. "Stamatíste. Ok, now go." I realized I was about to step into the shield she had created, which would probably not be good for my general health.

"Thanks." I told her. She nodded.

I turned, and saw Antheia on the floor. At least, I assumed it was Antheia. Everybody else blocked her.

"Come on, Antheia. Just a little longer. He should be here any second." I didn't wait for her response to Máni's disheartening encouragement.

"Piece on cloth, medium length, Resinæ ischyrá, at the double. Isabella, need some help here." I grabbed apiece of cloth Karus gave to me, and used it to stem the blood flow above the wound. I applied the balm and said, "Poú eínai i to dilitírio akómi paroúsa!" I studied the readings and took a deep calming breath.

Then I screamed.

"Why on earth didn't you all test her for venom residue?! Basilisk venom residue is as dangerous, if not more dangerous, than the actual venom! I taught you all the basics in case something like this was to happen! C'mon, guys! I-"

Isabella put her hand on my hand, and said, "What are the results?"

I took another deep breath. "There's not much time left."

"How long, exactly?" Antheia asked.

I bit my lips. "Four days, five at max." She nodded. I hesitated, and helped her to her feet. "Mystiká stin na apokalyftheí." There was a sort of shimmering around Antheia and me. I reached into my pocket and brought out a small vial.

"What-" She asked, confused.

"This is a transportation potion." I explained. "It takes the drinker to safety." I looked into her eyes. "Promise me that you will drink this if – no, *when* it becomes too dangerous. Go back to camp after three days and get the poison healed."

"I – I can't." She looked away.

"Look at me." I said fiercely. She reluctantly complied. "It's too dangerous. Camp will need every fighter it can possibly have. You *need* to become better." She stilled looked reluctant. "*I* need you to become better." I whispered. "I can't go on if – if I come close to losing you again." I confessed.

She hesitated. "I promise."

"In prima lingua," I demanded, my voice rough.

"Sou orkízomai na piei aftó elixírio metá epakrivós treis iméres." She said. I relaxed and smiled. I stepped away and was about to remove the spell, when Antheia reached over and took my hand. I smiled. "Stamatíste." She whispered. We stepped out into the Parthenon, hand in hand, and I was grinning like a madman.

XIII

Máni

We went into the Parthenon, and Antheia was spouting out some random facts to the rest of us.

"Antheia," I finally said, exasperated. "Nobody is listening! Would you please stop?"

She glared at me. Then she contacted me with her stone. *Listen, the only way we can get away with snooping around the base is if at least one of us acts a little studious and interested in the place.*

I internally smirked. *But you're not pretending.*

Her glare intensified, and I admit, I shrank away a little. She turned back to Helios, who was still holding her hand and grinning like an idiot. Wait, he is an idiot. "Where was I?" Antheia asked him.

"Something about the statue being chryse-something."

"Chryselephantine. The statue was built on a wooden base with thin carved slabs of ivory attached, representing the flesh, and sheets of gold leaf representing the garments, armor, hair, and other details. Sometimes, glass paste, glass, and precious and semi-precious stones were used for detail like eyes, jewelry, and weaponry."

Helios nodded, and then frowned. *How the hell are we supposed to get the lenses anyway?* He told all of us through the stone.

Language, Soliel! Antheia chastised.

Well, we need to get closer. Astrum said.

Antheia, will you do the honors?

"So, what happened to it?" Helios asked out loud.

Antheia smiled. "Well, some people said the Romans took it in the fifth century. In fact, an account mentions it in Constantinople in the tenth century AD. But basically, it disappeared."

Helios blinked, confused. "Disappeared?"

Antheia sighed. "For lack of a better word, yes, disappeared."

"Were there any carvings around the Athena Parthenos?"

She hesitated a little, and said, "I'm not sure." She looked frustrated. I wasn't sure if it was real or not, but it sure looked real. "I think there was something about Pandora or someone, but I can't remember."

Helios smiled. "Well, the best way to find out is to look at it!"

<hr>

After a lot of talking and coaxing and begging, we finally managed to convince the security to let us close to the base. Antheia was talking rapidly to Helios, and at the same time, communicating through the stone.

I don't know how she does it.

"...The birth of Pandora! The Gods created her to punish Prometheus. No, don't interrupt! Prometheus gave fire to mankind, which angered the gods..."

Máni, I need you to work on a spell to get us all below the pedestal without the security noticing that we are gone. I'll stay here since I'm the only one who knows about the Athena parthenos and the Parthenon and Pandora. Helios, go show yourself to the wolves and be ready to get us out of there, and alert camp if need be...

As I was saying, it was an impossible task.

We decided that I would start an illusion, and Antheia would maintain it. At the same time as the illusion, I would do an invisibility spell. Helios would do the same spell.

I scowled internally. I didn't understand why he couldn't let there be one spell. He said something about it being more difficult to handle one complex spell than two less complex spells. I tried arguing, but he said we could argue later, and for once, he was right.

I concentrated, and focused on the spell. I couldn't tell it out loud, for fear of the security noticing, but I had to get the spell to have a physical effect, and not just mentally. For this, I needed to do a spell in a mixture of Prima Lingua, the first Magical language, and El Lenguaje Magia, the latest magical language. It would also have a few stray words in other languages, but these two would be dominant.

I guess I've just given you a magical lesson.

Oh, well.

I did the spell, and the world dissolved.

Karus was the first to adjust to the darkness, and he let out a low whistle. "Whoa!" He said, turning around.

I blinked a couple of times, and whispered, "Oh. My. God."

"That has got to be the largest statue I've ever seen!" Astrum said. I just nodded, mesmerized.

In front of us was a forty-foot tall statue, and it was covered with precious things. Gold, ruby, diamond, sapphire, you name it, and it was there. I stepped back, and took in the whole statue. Something on Nike's wings caught my eye. "There! On the tip of her wings!" There was red lens on each pair. I told the guys, and turned to them. They nodded and took a step forward, and fell.

I screamed.

The ground had given way, and they had fallen down. Then, someone (or something) had cast a spell so that there was a barrier between the ground and what was beneath. The boys tried to climb up, but the barrier sent a sharp zap at them, and they fell back down. I could see that they were in dimly lit chambers, with a torch and a small chair. I yelled, "Stamatíste!" The barrier shuddered, flickered of, and reformed.

WHO DARES ENTER THE CHAMBER OF THE PARTHENOS?

I gulped, but stood my ground. "It is I, Máni of the Moon. May I know who I have the honor of addressing?"

I AM PROSTÁTIS, THE PROTECTOR! I AM THE GUARDIAN OF THE PARTHENOS! KNOW YOU NOT OF ME?

My mouth turned dry. "Of course, great Prostátes! I have heard much about you, but nothing I had heard prepared me for such greatness."

THEN LET ME ASK YOU, WHAT DO YOU WANT HERE?

Keep talking, I told myself. He likes it. "Oh illustrious one, my friends and I, we wish, no, need to take the lenses on Nike's wings for stopping Malvagita Ubella and his apprentice Cattiva Mauvaise from destroying camp."

AND HOW SHALL THIS HELP?

"The lenses alone have the power of helping us to gain the required knowledge. It is not otherwise possible."

YOU MAY TAKE THE LENSES, Prostátes said, and my heart leapt. *IF YOU ANSWER MY SEVEN RIDDLES.*

My heart sank. Riddles were Antheia's area, not mine! But ancient challenges were to be fought on by the person who was addressed, not by another.

IF YOU FAIL TO ANSWER ALL SEVEN, THEN YOU SHALL REMAIN HERE. IF YOU ANSWER ALL OF THEM, THEN CAN LEAVE WITH THE LENSES.

"May I take my friends with me?"

WHY WOULD I LET YOU DO THAT?

I stood straighter, deciding to take a gamble. "We are on a quest given to us by Der Estre Magier and Pas Oloi Elementa themselves."

There was a pause. I guess they were famous world wide, then. *THEN YOU MAY TAKE YOUR FRIENDS. BUT ANCIENT LAW STATES THAT YOU MUST ANSWER ALL SEVEN RIDDLES. IF AND ONLY IF YOU ANSWER THEM CAN YOU TAKE YOUR FRIENDS AND THE LENSES OUTSIDE THIS CAVERN.*

"What are is the first riddle?"

The air in front of me shimmered, and a man appeared. He was dressed in linen clothes, and had a short sword at his waist. He had a tan, and an Elementa amulet. He gave me a short bow. "I am Prostátes. Here is your riddle:

> *I am greater than god.*
> *I am more evil than the devil.*
> *The poor have me,*
> *The rich need me,*
> *And death comes to those who eat me.*
> *Who am I?"*

I frowned, confused. What could possibly be good and evil at the same time? Nothing can be greater than god, and nothing can be more evil than the devil- hang on.

Nothing is greater than god.

Nothing is more evil than the devil.

The poor have practically nothing.

The rich need practically nothing.

You die if you eat nothing.

All check. I looked up and told Prostátes. "The answer is nothing."

He smiled. "Riddle me this, she of the Moon:

> *I am ever hungry,*
> *And live if you feed me.*
> *I am never thirsty,*
> *And die if you quench me.*
> *What am I?"*

This was an easy one, I realized. "Fire." I replied.
"Then tell me, Mond:

> *I see much, but change little.*
> *I am firm, irresolute,*
> *Powerful, but gentle;*
> *I have enough strength to rip apart mountains,*
> *Yet be moved by gentle stirrings,*
> *I am life itself,*
> *And I give life to others.*
> *Who am I?*

I thought about it, and realized this was another easy one. "A tree."
"Well, moonlight, answer this:

> *I'm a five letter word that has no end,*
> *One through three can amend,*
> *One, four and five are something alive,*
> *Two and three occur near thee.*
> *What am I?"*

This was a word puzzle. Words that have no end...infinity, infinite,
endless...Some*thing* that has no end...stars. But sta doesn't mean make

amends…Abyss? Aby…it exists, but not sure what it means. Ass is a donkey, a living thing. By, nearby. I decided to take the chance. "Abyss."

He smiled. "Well, then,

> *I am light as a feather,*
> *Yet no man can hold me for long.*
> *My presence causes life,*
> *My absence death.*

What am I?"

I smiled. "Breath."

> *"I welcome the day with a show of light,*
> *I steathily came here in the night.*
> *I bathe the earthy stuff at dawn,*
> *But by the noon, alas! I'm gone."*

I nearly said shadow, but I stopped myself (just in time). Shadows don't bathe anything, that would be soap or water. What comes in the morning and goes by noon? I smiled again. "Dew."

> *"The last, but not the least, little one:*
> *Lighter than what I am made of,*
> *More of me is hidden than is seen,*
> *I am the bane of the mariner,*
> *A tooth within the sea.*
> *Speak my name.*

Bane of the mariner…There's a poem "Rime of the Ancient Mariner". So, is the bane the Albatross? But that doesn't fulfill any of the other conditions. The mariner went to the "land of mist and snow", and snow is ice. Icebergs are only partly seen, about one-tenth. "Ice."

Prostátes extended his arm. "Take it." On his palm lay the lenses. I reached out, and it floated towards me. A moment later, he disappeared, and Karus and Astrum appeared beside me. The lenses floated towards Astrum and he took it. He looked at it, and we saw an ocean, and a lot of coral. "The great barrier reef." Astrum breathed, enthralled.

"Wonderful," I snapped. "Let's get out of here, and then you can do whatever you need to do." We transported to the Parthenon, and relayed the events to the others.

XIV

Máni

"So the next location is-"

"The great barrier reef."

Helios looked annoyed, but when he spoke, his voice was level. "We *just* came back from there. We could have just taken the lens, if it were the next location!"

"No, Helios. Remember what Bianca told us?" Antheia told him.

"Wha- Oh, yeah." He glanced at Antheia, sheepish. "Forgot."

"Evidently." I snapped. The others looked at me. "We need to get a move on!" I said, glaring at them. *Then* they had the decency to look sheepish. Helios however, looked up and pursed his lips.

"Well, I need to eat first! I'm starving!"

Antheia and I exchanged glances. "When was the last time you ate?" Antheia asked.

Helios thought about it, and then his eyes widened. "No wonder I'm so hungry. I ate before the Jorōgumo incident."

I glared at him. Then I did a little spell that I discovered a few months back. No, it did not summon food. It created just enough space in the air for emergency supplies – a bow and quiver of arrows, twin daggers, and, most importantly, some food. The food was just some bread wrapped in cling wrap, and I replaced it every two days. I grabbed the bread and gave it to him. "We'll get some more food after we get the lenses. It should be easier than the previous ones, since there's not going to be any Darkness."

Helios took the bread. "Not sure about that," he said, taking a bite. "I did a balanced spell with Bella."

I raised my eyebrows questioningly, and mouthed, *Bella?* My question was answered a moment later when Isabella reached out and slapped the back of his head. "Don't call me Bella. Only Ells can call me that."

"Ells? Oh, Bianca. Sorry." My dimwitted friend replied. I laughed and shook my head. Then, I summoned the wall, and we went to Australia.

As it turned out, I was right. We did *not* have to do much, but I wasn't sure about the balance. It seemed more like one-is-to-one than two-is-to-one. I shrugged it off, and went with the others to get the lenses. This time it went to Helios. These lenses were sea green. I thought it was 'cause it was under the sea, or maybe it was under the sea because it was sea green.

Whatever.

We stopped in Australia for the day, and got some food (Ah, amazing food). Helios ate like there was no tomorrow. Helios and I then took guard in wolf form, and Isabella helped disguise us.

So, how's things been in the pack? Helios asked.

Oh, so now you ask. He waited. I sighed. *We found one of the wolves with the mark of Mors.*

WHAT?!

We found –

Yeah, I heard. But how? The spell we did was powerful enough to remove it.

Yes, but he hid it. He had no choice, and we made sure he wouldn't use his powers against us.

I need to talk to him.

Do it later. We need to complete this shift, and you *need rest.*

He nodded. We spent the rest of the shift in silence.

XV

Antheia

The next day, Isabella took her leave. "I need to help my sister," she had said.

We started late after that. The next place was the Great Wall of China. We got there with no problem. That's the good news. The bad news? The whole wall was Dark, and it was evenly spread. We had no way of knowing which part of the wall the lenses would be in. That wouldn't be a problem, except there was a spell that prevented any of the usual spells from helping us do anything. Basically, we needed a dark spell. Helios and Máni had a silent conversation. Then Helios said, "Skoteinó." A werewolf with dark brown fur came to us. Suddenly, Astrum hissed.

"The mark of Mors!" he said, and glared at Máni and Helios.

"What!" I demanded, and looked at the wolf's back. There, in black on its fur, lay the mark of Mors.

I drew my spear. Máni and Helios formed a V in front of the wolf. "Explain." I growled, giving them my 'it-better-be-good' glare. "You have one minute."

Helios turned to the wolf. "Transform, Skoteinó." The wolf transformed into a boy with emerald green eyes, and black hair. He was rather pale, but looked strong. I raised my eyebrows.

"I used to be a white Elemental. Gems. Emeralds were my speciality." He nodded towards Karus, who had eyes like yellow topaz. I guessed that that was his speciality. "I got bitten on my amulet, so it appeared as the Mark of Mors when I transformed. I did a spell to make it appear as the mark of Mors anyway, but I obviously didn't show it off."

I glared at him, still suspicious. "Open your mind." I ordered. He glanced at Helios, who gave a slight nod. He lowered his mind barriers, and I glanced through his memories.

He was in a high position in Daniel Wolf's pack, but he wanted to leave the pack. The problem was that those who left the pack were usually killed. The only way they could leave safely was if Luna came, and that was near impossible. He was also used by Malvagita and Cattiva as a tool, and he got the feeling they used him only if it was probably not safe. Wolf also treated him as dispensible. He'd been waiting for Helios to come back, when the rule was passed. Then, he knew it was done to prevent any more desertions, in preparation for the upcoming war.

They'd been selecting people at random, but only males, to join the pack. He had to do several of them, and he had apologised to them in private. He finally got to leave the pack, and he took it with both hands.

At this I got out, and relaxed my position. I indicated that the others do so.

"What's your Elemental name?" Karus asked, curius.

Skoteinó smiled. "Smeraldo Kostbare."

"Emerald. Mine's topaz. I can do most varieties, but Yellow topaz is best."

"I do Ruby pretty good too, but, yeah, Emerald."

"Have you-"

"Guys!" Máni and I shouted at the same time. "Do your thing later." Máni continued. "Smeraldo – can I call you Smeraldo? Thanks – we called you to see if you can do a Dark locate spell."

He nodded and turned to the wall. Then he smiled. "I was here. I did this part of the wall, but there were different people who did different things."

"Just do the spell!" I snapped.

"Sheesh. Entopíste." There was no change, but Smeraldo said, "Follow me." Then he walked through the wall. Helios and Máni followed him without hesitation. The rest of us glanced at each other. I shrugged and went in. Then, everything went black.

———⊰⊱———

I sat up groggily. What happened? I remembered the Parthenon, the riddles, China, the Wolf! I shot up. *I have to go help the others. I have to get out of here. Wait, where is here?*

I looked around, and found myself in a dark room. I tried to find if it was magically dark, but I couldn't tell. I couldn't feel any of my magic. There was something, but I couldn't access it.

Panic clogged up my throat. I hadn't been without magic for like, two years! I started hyperventilating, then took a deep breath. Panic would do none of us any good. I tried reaching the others with my stone, with no luck. Then I tried a balanced spell for lighting up the room. Again, no – wait. There was something, a flicker, something. I tilted my head and thought about it.

Communication stone did not work.

Identification spell didn't work.

Balanced light spell – sort of worked.

I nearly panicked again. The first two were all White. The balanced spell had a bit of Dark in it. White doesn't work.

I had to do Dark spells to get to the others.

XVI

Antheia

I started panicking. I didn't know any dark spells, and I didn't wand to taint my amulet (or myself). I thought I could do a powerful balance spell, but I would lose precious energy. I thought about it for a bit and then sighed. *Stuck between a rock and a hard place.* Then I bit my lip, and did one of the few Dark spells that I know – to break the wall in front of me. "Thrymmatízo!" Shatter!

The wall collapsed. The spell was more powerful than what I had intended, but I shrugged. Then I walked out, and found myself in a corridor. I looked around, and lo and behold! The others were there. "Helios and Máni got us out. Smeraldo was going to get you out when you blasted the wall so spectacularly." I glared in the general direction of the speaker, but I couldn't identify him. I turned to Smeraldo, who was right next to me.

"I don't suppose you can light up this thing?" I asked.

He smiled and summoned a gem. Then he murmured something, and the whole corridor lit up green.

"Creepy." Astrum shuddered. Then, the green mixed with blue, and Astrum jumped. Karus smiled, holding a blue gem. I guessed it was Topaz.

"It's a general spell. Neither light, nor dark."

I summoned a ruby. "Tell me."

"Whoa!" Smeraldo said, stepping back. "How on earth did you do that?"

"Practice. What's the spell?"

"Thermiká."

I repeated that, and the room turned red. The other colors were suppressed.

"Tone it down a little!" Karus yelled.

I concentrated, and the red dimmed. Then, it blended with the other colors and formed white. "That's a lot less creepy." Astrum said, grinning. I slapped the back of his head, and he said, "Ow!" rubbing his head.

I rolled my eyes, and told Smeraldo, "Lead on."

———— ✦ ————

In five minutes, our gems dimmed, and we found ourselves in front of a black mist. "What's this?" I demanded. Smeraldo transformed and sniffed the air. Máni and Helios stiffened and transformed. "What?" I demanded, scowling.

It's the Mist of Sorrow, the Mist of Hardship, the Mist of Anger, the Mist of Dark. It stands for all things bad, all feelings dark. It shows us what we fear the most, and tries to drive us insane. Helios told us through mind speech. Then he transformed, put up privacy charms, and said, "Will you have the potion now?" He sounded hopeful. I shook my head. He sighed. "Just remember, nothing it shows is ever true. It changes little things nagging the back of your head to visions very real." He hesitated, and then leaned forward. He kissed my forehead, and said, "Good luck." He cancelled the privacy charms and transformed. "Let's go, guys. We need to hurry. Never believe what it shows, even if it seems real. It never is." I said.

The wolves leapt into the fog, with Helios at the head, Máni on the right and a step behind, and Smeraldo on the left and two steps behind. I glanced at the others, and stepped into the fog.

Immediately, my arm began burning. I glanced at it, and I saw my basilisk wound, infected. I took a deep breath and thought about how my arm was before I went in. The pain faded, and I moved on.

I saw various visions all around me, of Camp burning, of my fellow Jeunes dying, of the five of us failing, of Bianca getting stabbed, but I move on resolutely. *Not real,* I thought. *Not real.*

I don't know how long I had been in there for, but the fog began to thin. I looked forward, and saw the lenses in the center of the room. Helios and Máni were already there and they were hugging, and smiling. Helios seemed happy with her. I thought he liked me, but it turned out he liked Máni. I took a deep breath and was about to scream, when something caught my eye. There was no amulet on their hands. *Not real.* I sighed in relief, and almost immediately, the fog came forward and surrounded me again.

I went on, and finally saw a faint glow. There was a pair of lenses, and the fog was thickest around it. Near it, I saw three wolves – White, silver, and brown. I moved forward, but it was like walking through oil. The fog felt oppressive, and I couldn't breath. I tried harder, but with no avail. Finally, Smeraldo stamped his foot. The darkness got expelled, and I fell forward. Immediately, the white wolf came next to me, and helped me up. I smiled at it. "Helios." I turned my attention back to the lenses, where Smeraldo was sniffing. Apparently he must have sent some message to Helios, because he transformed and drew his spear. *Call the others.* He told me through MindSpeech. I nodded.

Guys, come on. I called. I know, lame. But in my defense, I wanted them quick, and they always tried to find openings to try to insult me in a friendly way, though mostly without success.

Of course, it worked, and Astrum and Karus came a minute later. *Take your spears,* Helios ordered. *We need to do a balance spell to get them. There's too much Dark. He's gotten more paranoid, I guess.*

I took my spear, and then filled it with my power (Yes, we can store power in them. Long story). Then I frowned. *We can't get any mist.*

Yes, we can. Try again. I hesitated, and extended my arm. I thought about the mist, and it came. I filled my spear, and went to my position. *It's uneven. We need another Elemental with another spear.*

We have another Elemental. Astrum said.

The five of us walked towards each other simultaneously. Karus summoned a diamond, as perfect as the one on the rest of the spears. I extended my arm, and managed to summon enough gold for the shaft. Astrum shaped it, with three chambers (Don't waste your breath – check the records), and handed the shaft to Helios. He attached the diamond to the shaft, and handed it to Máni. She did the spells on the spear, and went to Smeraldo. "Transform, Skoteinó."

He transformed into Human form. "I give you this spear, Skoteinó Smeraldo Kostbare Lÿkos. Use it well."

I widened my eyes. A formal offering – that ensured that he wouldn't betray us. Provided he accepted it.

He eyed Máni warily. Then he reached out and firmly grasped the spear with his right hand. "I accept, Lupa Máni Mond Lÿkos." He took the spear, and ran his finger along the shaft. "I name thee Praesul, Protector of the Elementals." The spear tip glowed, as did all of ours. His voice resonated in all of our bodies, and I guessed that all our spears were named Praesul now.

Máni started saying, "You need-"

"I know. We do not have much time." He said. Máni nodded and took her position. I went to mine, and pointed it right at the lenses. Then I took a deep breath, and, at the same time, we began.

We'd done this spell before (Don't ask), so it wasn't difficult. As the spell finished, there was a mini-White explosion, and a lot of dark was banished. There was perfect balance. I smiled, and stepped forward. The lenses floated up, and we followed its progress. It went to Smeraldo, and he took it. These lenses worried me. It was black, and seemed opaque, but it was actually transparent (sort of). Smeraldo saw the lenses, and we waited. He turned to us. "The next location is the Sphinx."

I nodded, and stepped forward. The next moment, I blacked out.

The last thing that I thought was, *Great, out twice in a day. That's a record.*

XVII

Karus

The moment Antheia fell, Helios came to here side. He murmured, "Poú eínai i to dilitírio akómi paroúsa." He became still for a moment, and then took a deep breath. "Does anyone have a piece of paper?"

I nodded and handed it over. "Why-"

"Pen." He snapped, not wanting to talk. I handed it over, and he scribbled something on the paper. He tore it, and stuffed it into her pocket. He wrote something else on the other bit of paper, and stuck it in her jacket so it sticks out. Then, from her jacket pocket, he took a vial, and gently poured the contents into her throat. He stepped back, and a warm glow surrounded her. I turned away, but I think Helios looked on. When I looked again, she was gone.

Helios said two words. "Transporter potion."

I nodded. "Bad?" Astrum asked.

Helios reluctantly nodded. "Sent her to camp. They can heal her."

I nodded, and turned to Smeraldo. "Looks like you're gonna be part of this quest, bro."

He shook his head. "No wolf is allowed to take part in a quest unless he or she is an alpha or second in command."

I pursed my lips. "Unofficial part, then."

He smiled. "I guess."

"Where's Isabella?" Máni asked.

"She transported to camp." Helios said.

Máni sighed. "On a quest with only boys. Just my luck."

Helios smiled slightly. "Well, Mond, think you're up to it?"

She glared at him. "Are you?" She retorted.

"You sound like Isabella."

"Picked up the habit from years of being with her as Katherine."

They shared a smile and turned to us. "Lets get moving."

We got to the sphinx no problem. We knew where the lenses were immediately.

The problem? We ran into some Egyptian Elementals immediately, and none of us knew Egyptian.

"We," I said, gesturing wildly, "Quest."

"El nar," One of them said, showing their amulet. Then he pointed to us. "Min?"

There were two guys and a girl. The guy had fiery red hair and fierce eyes. The other had black hair and deep blue eyes. I guessed the first was fire and the secont was water. The girl seemed to be an Elemental, with long black hair and multicolored eyes.

I showed my amulet. "Gems." I said. Then I frowned. "Hold on." I wondered if they knew Prima Lingua. "Aftó eínai Astrum, Máni, Smeraldo kai Helios. Ego Karus."

The girl smiled. "Hello, Astrum, Máni, Smeraldo, Helios, Karus." She said in Prima Lingua. "I am Et de Lúmine, Elementa. These two are Pÿros and Sobek, Fire and water Elementals respectively. Why are you here?"

"We're on a quest. You know Malvagita and Cattiva, don't you?"

"Yes, We're trying to fight an attack."

"So are we. We're looking for lenses like these." Helios extended his hand.

She frowned. "We have one like this." Sobek said. "We are using it. We need it."

"May we see it?"

He hesitated, glancing at the girl. She extended her arm, and we saw the pair on her wrist. It seemed opaque white, but closer observation showed that we could see through it.

I hesitated, torn between loyalties to Camp and need to help all Elementals. Then I did a communication spell. Bianca and Albus were dueling, again. This time, however, neither of them held back. They cast random spells, and went so fast, I couldn't keep track of them. Finally, the duel ended like all others. Bianca had Albus pinned to the ground with one of her swords at his neck.

"Stren!" She yelled.

"Guys!" We yelled. "We have a situation." I spoke in prima lingua.

"Right." Bianca did a quick spell, and her clothes neatened out immediately. She made a short bow, and pulled Albus to do the same. "A pleasure to meet you, Et de Lúmine," She said.

"How do you know my name?"

"Estre." She gestured vaguely to her head.

"Ah." Et de Lúmine bowed. "Call me Lúmine. Perhaps we can form a temporary alliance against the Dark?"

Bianca smiled dryly. "We cannot completely vanquish it. A balance needs to be maintained."

Lúmine nodded. "True. As long as we can keep it up?"

Bianca nodded. "I think it would be appropriate. I am Bianca Luminis, and this is my second in command, Albus Patronus." She shot him a look, and must have told something through MindSpeech, because he looked sheepish.

"About the lenses." Lúmine said. "We found this pair in the sphinx, protected by Dark magic. It has helped us read many of our scrolls. However, I think we are missing a lot of knowledge."

"Let us share the knowledge, then. We have seven pairs now – Antheia is OK, by the way – and we can read quite a bit. But it's a bit weird."

"I see what you mean."

Máni had been standing in a corner silently, till now. "Did the Lenses come to you?"

"No, they were floating in mid air. I took it."

"Karus, extend your arm." Then she turned to the Egyptians. "The lenses had floated to one of us when we went near it. That's how we managed to get five pairs." Lúmine nodded, like it made sense. I extended my arm, and the lenses detached itself from her arm. It attached itself to mine, and I brought it closer. I Saw a lot of colors, and a lot of snow. "Aurora Borealis." I breathed. "It's beautiful."

"Go." Lúmine said. "Send us a message when you get anymore knowledge." She told Bianca.

"We will." She said, and cut the connection.

"Are you sure?" I asked.

She nodded. "It is necessary. I wish you luck on your quest."

"You need it." Pÿros shook our hands.

"Wish you all luck as well." We bowed, and turned away.

"Let's find some place to stay." Máni said.

Pÿros yelled, "When's the deadline?"

"Two more days!" I yelled back. "Two more Locations!"

"Then stay the night!" Lúmine yelled.

We glanced at each other, shrugged, and went back with them.

XVIII

Karus

The Egyptian camp was…different, to say the least. It was familiar, and different at the same time.

There was no division on basis of amulets. In fact, there was no official division. However, everyone treated Lúmine as the leader, and it was obvious that Pÿros and Sobek were closest to her.

There were few campers, and by that, I mean twenty campers. It seemed very small, but it must have been necessary.

Our camp was on a different dimension, so to speak. We basically shifted our base so it was in the same place in a parallel world. If we summoned the Wall without specifying a place, we could end up in a completely different world. Confused? Me too.

This camp, however, was on the same base, and had no magical protections. The campers seemed to be wary, but trusted us (more or less) since we came with Lúmine. However, I had a feeling they would sleep better when we left.

I turned to Lúmine. "Why are there so few Elementals?"

Her expression turned dark. "We lost them to Malvagita and Cattiva."

I stayed silent. What kind of response could you give to such a statement?

"How many did you lose?" She asked after some time.

"None. Bianca and Albus – the people you saw in the message – challenged those two to a duel. Malvagita, as the challenged, set the terms for the duel, and changed it to a double duel. Bianca and Albus killed them, but it turns out they didn't die after all."

She was silent for a while. "We lost nearly twenty people. That was a little under half of the people in camp. Then few were killed individually."

"Why don't you shift to another dimension?"

"We don't know where we'll end up."

"Magical protections?"

"We need more Elementals to do that."

"We could help."

"Still won't be enough."

"We know a spell to make it enough." Astrum said, entering the conversation.

Her eyes lit up. "Really? When can we do it?"

"Sunset. When there is perfect balance."

"But its so easy to tip the balance then," she whispered.

"We've done quite a few balanced spells, two of them with our spears."

"With your *what*?"

"Spears." Máni came up. "Anima Tueur on that hill over there. Hidden, but I know its there. Helios and Smeraldo have gone to handle it, but I think backup would be good."

"Let's go, then."

"Hang on, we can't kill it!" Lúmine yelled.

We looked at her weirdly. "You need to stab it in the heart and head, at the same time or in the same second." Astrum said.

I saw Máni raise her eyebrows. Astrum shook his head. Suddenly, Helios contacted me. *Back up needed! There are three!*

I cursed and started sprinting towards them. I vaguely heard Máni tell Lúmine what Helios had said. I just kept running.

I drew by spear when I got there, and yelled, "Elementis!" My spear tip glowed, and I sent a bolt of energy at one of the Anima Tueurs. It fell back, and Máni stabbed it in the heart. I went forward and stabbed it in the head, but I was a millisecond too late. It got up and tossed Máni aside. She sat up groggily. I whispered, "Stamatíste." I drew my swords, and heard Máni murmur a spell. I slashed my blades while yelling, "Elementa!" I gave the Anima Tueur a good sized cut, and leapt forward. This time, I managed to kill it.

I turned, and saw that the others had dealt with the rest of them.

"Elements?" Lúmine asked.

"Gives the power of the Elements to the required thing, as long as it is non – living." I said, taking deep breaths. "Try it."

She yelled, "Elementa!" Her sword glowed really bright, and she slashed the air in front of her. "How do I end it?"

"Stop."

"Stamatíste!" The glowing dimmed, and then shut off completely.

"Are there any more?" I asked.

"No. We thank you." She said, bowing. I bowed back, and sheathed my swords.

"Is anybody else hungry?" I asked, and my friends yelled an affirmative. Lúmine just looked at us weirdly. "On a quest, remember?" I said, grinning.

She rolled her eyes and gestured that we follow her. She took us to a large round table, and made us sit next to her. She made a few announcements, and then told them, "As you can see, we have a few guests today. These are Máni Mond, Helios Soliel, Karus Kostbare,

Smeraldo Kostbare, and Astrum Estrella. They killed the Anima Tueurs today." She had to stop because there was a loud cheer from around the table. "They will be staying here for the night. At sunset, they have offered us help in putting up wards. They are on a quest to find these." Here, she gestured to my hand, and there were many sounds of outrage. "Silence!" She bellowed, and the group instantly quieted down. "We have established contact with the Leaders in the other camp, and we have agreed to help each other."

Some kid shouted something in Arabic, and scowled. "It is necessary." She said, pursing her lips. "That's all today from here. Is there anything else?"

Another girl got up from the other end. "There's the small matter of the Werewolves we found."

"What color, and what type?" Helios demanded.

The girl glared at him. He didn't back down. "They were brown, or grey. They must be Dark, because, what other type of werewolf is there?"

"White." Máni said, simply.

"You lie!" The girl spat.

"No. It is possible. There are white werewolves. In fact, there is a white pack of werewolves."

"I do not believe you." The girl said.

"Listen here, girlie," Máni started.

"Sarah Estrella." She snapped.

"Whatever, star-struck. I said that in Prima Lingua. A little heads up – you can't lie in Prima Lingua."

"You lie!" Way to repeat, girlie.

"You try lying in Prima Lingua then, kid."

She opened her mouth, but no sound came out. She tried again, with no success. "How do you know?" She demanded.

Helios and Smeraldo stood up. "I have another name. Lupus Lÿkos."

"I am Skoteinó Lÿkos."

"I am Lupa Lÿkos."

They transformed simultaneously, and showed off their marks. "Skoteinó is dark."

Máni bared her teeth. *No, he isn't. Get your facts straight.*

"Then why does he have the Mark of Mors on his fur?"

Look below it, dummy.

I hid a smile. Looked like Máni has a rival. "Oh." Sarah said. She sat back, sheepish. Below the mark of Mors, there was a white patch of fur. It seemed like nothing, but it was enough to prove that he was a White werewolf.

The three of them transformed again, and Helios said, "It's probably my pack. Are they bothering you?"

"No." Lúmine answered. Helios tilted his head. Máni nodded, once.

Helios turned to Lúmine. "What do you feel about having some of them as a little help?"

Lúmine turned to the rest of the Elementals. "All against accepting this offer?"

Three people raised their hands, Sarah among them. I noticed Astrum looking at her in disgust. "All in favor of accepting this offer?"

Everybody else raised their hands. "We accept this generous offer." She told him, and he grinned.

"Legatum!" Helios called, and a moment later, a grey wolf bounded to him. "Select ten?" He turned to Lúmine, and she nodded. "Select ten other wolves and stay back with these Elementals. Help them out with whatever necessary. Clear?"

The wolf nodded and bounded away. We ate the rest of the meal in silence. Then Helios got up. "Time to do the spell, right?"

The five of us got up and told Lúmine to direct us to the center of camp. We did the spell in a few minutes, and just in time too. Then, we decided to crash.

XIX

Astrum

The next morning, we left the camp with some supplies – food, clothes, energy storing crystal, healing potion, Resinæ, spare dagger – what you'd probably need in a quest. We left the camp after teaching the Elementals communication spell. I summoned the wall, and we got to the Arctic ocean.

Let me fill you in about the Aurora. Here's what you've heard about the aurora: An aurora is a natural light display in the sky that occurs particularly in the high latitude regions, and is caused by the collision of energetic charged particles with atoms in the high altitude atmosphere.

Here's what it actually is. There was this Elemental, named Aurora (Yes, what did you expect?) Soliel. There was a feud of sorts between the Elementals of the Camps. A division seemed eminent. Some were trying to ease the tension, but it never worked. They were so few in number that no one paid attention to them. Finally, Aurora got very annoyed at them for fighting and ignoring her that her magic exploded. She wove a complex spell without speaking (Yes, it is difficult), and created the Aurora. It is suppose to reflect the severity of the situation with Elementals. Basically, if there's going to be a drastic decrease in the numbers, the Aurora will be red. If things are peaceful, it will be green. The color everyone looks forward to is purple – perfect situation. Blue is between green and purple. Yellow is between red and green, towards green. Pink is more towards red.

The Elementas are supposed to go there once a year to check the situation, and usually, the reports say green. Some reports say blue, but that's very rare. I guessed Bianca, Albus, Juliet (the previous Elementa), and Lúmine were saved a trip to the cold.

And boy was it freezing. We were stumbling around the snow, trying to unfreeze our brains and try and think where the Lenses would be. Finally, I gave up and said, "Thermótita." Heat.

"Awesome!" Máni said, edging closer. Helios transformed, as did Smeraldo. "Why didn't I think of that?" She murmured, and transformed. We looked up at the Aurora, and immediately, I got confused.

There was a band of green, a band of red, and a small band of purple. Weird. "Are you seeing what I'm seeing?" I asked.

"Contrasting colors? Yeah." I didn't see who said that, but I bet it was Karus. The other three were in wolf form.

I stared at it, and froze (Not literally.). "Mýga." Fly. I shot up, and saw it clearly. "Guys," I yelled down. "The lenses are here!"

Karus flew up immediately. The wolves came up in wolf form. Karus cursed, and said, "How will we get it now?"

I smiled and did a little nonverbal spell I had been working on. I summoned a bit of mist, at a bit of my stellar essence, and a few others. Then, I gently blew it towards the lenses. It floated there, and then floated back with the lenses in its center. They stayed there, and then flashed to Máni. I grinned at her. "Congratulations on being the only person to get two pairs."

She flashed a smile and said, "Thanks." She observed the lenses again, and glared at it. Helios relayed the info to me through

MindSpeech, and I nearly cursed. The runes were in Prima Lingua, bit that wasn't the bad bit.

The runes said:

The Great Library of Alexandria.

I cursed.

XX

Astrum

"I already told you why it's practically impossible!" I yelled at Karus.

"Give me the short and simple version." He snapped.

I took a deep breath. "The library was burnt down. The scrolls were lost. Burnt to ashes. No one knows who did it, but it was done. The scroll might not even exist now!"

Smeraldo spoke. "Maybe we should ask Lúmine."

I froze. Why didn't I think of that? Oh, right. I was busy panicking and explaining to Karus. I nodded and sent Lúmine a message.

"Hey, in a situation here." I said.

"Yes?" She asked, frowning a bit.

"We've gotten all the lenses, but the scroll is/was is the Great Library of Alexandria."

"How do you know?" She gave me her full attention now, scowling.

"We See the next location in the lenses. We didn't See this one, but we Saw the words in Prima Lingua."

She was silent for a bit. Then she sighed. "Come over for a day. We'll se what we can do."

I nodded my thanks and cut the connection. We summoned the wall and transported there.

———◆———

"Do you know where it might be?" Karus asked Lúmine.

We'd been trying to get information from her, with no avail. She hadn't spoken a word since she told us, "Come," as soon as we arrived.

Finally, I snapped. I grabbed her hand and pulled her to a stop. I glared at her and said, "Listen, Et de Lúmine. The fate of both Light *and* Life hangs on the fate of this quest. If you can help us, now would be a good time to mention it. If not, well, we know the way out."

She stared at me for a few seconds, and sighed. "Come."

I didn't move. "Don't you care?" Máni demanded. "It needs to be put together! There's a lot of magic in there, and if we don't do this fast, the whole world might explode, if not more!"

Lúmine froze. I turned to Máni. "How do you know?" I demanded. "I can't feel a thing!"

She hesitated. "It's like this buzzing sensation in the back of my head, kind of like what we feel when we try to sense magic. If I try to listen to it, its like my head is going to burst. I remembered Lau telling me something the Seven found while doing some research. She told me how to find the degree of magic that we sense, and this was the second level."

"What's the first level?" Smeraldo asked.

"Sensing is like your whole body is burning if you try to listen. Level...universe will get destroyed."

"Éla." Lúmine said, and the world turned upside down.

We had transported to a chamber, and it was *old*. I turned to Lúmine. "What is this place?" I demanded roughly.

"The chamber of-"

"The ancients." We whirled round.

"Der- Der Estre Magier?" Helios stammered, stunned. "Pas Oloi Elementa?" He turned to the other figure in the room.

They both had black hair and ever-changing eyes, like the Aurora. They were dressed in ancient clothes. Estre was wearing a simple white dress, with a V-neck and long sleeves. She wore simple flat foot shoes. On her right hand there was an Elementa Amulet, and on her left hand, there was a golden bracelet. At her waist was a ceremonial dagger, and in her hair was a golden circlet, symbolizing the leadership of the Elementals.

To her left stood Pas, with a simple crown on his head, also symbolizing leadership of Elementals. He was wearing a white tunic and white pants with black boots (did boots exist then?). At his waist was another ceremonial dagger.

There were more Elementals around them, but I didn't wait to see them. As one, the six of us knelt, drawing our spears.

"Rise, Elementals. Welcome." Estre spoke, her voice musical. We rose, and stared around us in wonder. The Chamber of the Ancients… it was beautiful.

"Welcome, Antheia Jeune." Helios turned faster than what must have been good for his health.

"Antheia," he breathed, and stepped forward. Antheia rose and ran towards him. He murmured something in her ear, and she nodded. The separated and turned towards the Ancients.

"We thank you, Et de Lúmine." Pas said, his deep voice echoing around the chamber. There was a flash of light, and she was gone.

"Lupus Helios Soliel Lÿkos, step forward." Helios went forward. "We have decided to give you a gift. You have long shown an aptitude for healing, and now you shall have the Gift. Do you accept?"

"I do." He said with a little difficulty.

"Then extend your arm."

Helios stepped forward, knelt, and extended his arm. Pas touched his hand with a finger, and a mark appeared on Helios' arm. It was a simple one, a triangle within a circle. "Use it well, Giatró." He also got the title of Amólyntos, the first Wolf.

Helios rose and stepped back. Next, Estre called, "Antheia Jeune, come forth." She got a beautiful sword, named Bellator, the warrior. I didn't get an opportunity to examine it, and swore I would when I did. She too got the name Bellator.

"Astrum Estrella." Pas called. "You have the make of a strategist. Yet you have no opportunity to hone this talent. I give you Sapientia, Wisdom and Knowledge." He touched my arm and gave me a small mark. It was a grey ellipse, filled in. I bowed and stepped back, now called Consilium.

Next he called Karus. He became Placo, Peace. He was to be ambassador of Elementals, and keep peace between them.

Next Estre called Máni. She became Artemis, the Huntress, and was given a bow that would never miss, and a quiver that would never run out. It was silver, but it didn't hurt her. Then she was given the title Prima Lýkaina, the first She-wolf.

Finally, they called Smeraldo. "Skoteinó Smeraldo Kostbare Lÿkos, you have done your best to maintain the Balance, and have succeeded. We ask you to stay and continue doing so from here. Lÿkos, do you wish to join the ranks of the Ancients?"

They were greeted by a stunned silence. Then, somehow, Smeraldo managed to get out, "Yes." Immediately, a bright light engulfed the room. I closed my eyes, and when I opened them, we were in Camp. I mean, home.

"Guys?" We whirled round, and came face to face with Bianca.

"Hi, Bianca." I said. Then I extended my arm, and indicated that the others do the same. "Eamus!" I yelled. Join. The lenses floated off our hands, and joined. It became a single pair of lenses. As I watched, it joined with others that floated off a string from Bianca's neck. Then, it became a pair of spectacles, and floated to me. I handed it to Bianca. "Here you go."

She smiled. "Thanks, Consilium. And by the way, not Bianca, Hemera."

"Hi! Oh, wow!" Albus came up from behind us. I turned around, and saw that we were on one of the leaf walls (long story). "Is it your shift?" I asked Bianca – no, Hemera.

"Nope. Just came here and checked the situation."

I nodded, and grinned. "How's training?" I asked, grinning at Albus."

"Great!" Albus said, the same moment Hemera said, "Horrid!"

They went into one of their mini arguments again, and something caught my ear – Iskios. Shadow.

"Iskios?" I said, drawing them out of their argument.

"Yeah, Iskios Albus Stren Elementa Patronus Kynigós. Huge, and a mouthful, I know."

Shadow Hunter. Iskios Kynigós. Apt, somehow.

Bianca slapped the back of his head and said, "Hemera Bianca Ella Elementa Luminis Komistís." She bowed.

"Consilium Astrum Estrella Sapientia." I said, bowing a little.

"Bellator Antheia Jeune Proelia." Antheia followed suit.

"Placo Karus Kostbare Eiríni." Karus came up next.

"Giatró Amólyntos Lupus Helios Soliel Lÿkos Giátrissa."

"Artemis Lupa Máni Mond Lÿkos Giátrissa Cacciatrix."

We waited, and then realized Smeraldo wasn't there. We stepped back, but didn't worry. He was an Ancient now.

Hemera held up her lenses and smiled. "Time to read."

XXI

Antheia

Lets go back a bit, to when I collapsed in China. When I woke up, I was in a room with white curtains and a warm, calming look. I sat up, and felt dizzy immediately. I fell back.

"Easy, there." I whirled towards the speaker, knife in hand. "Whoa!" She stepped back, hands raised.

"Lau?" I asked, my throat raw. "Lau Mond?"

"The very same." She grinned. A moment later, Bianca strolled in. "Got your message," she said, nodding at Lau.

"I'm back in camp?" I asked, confused.

"Yeah. You came here with a transporter potion, with basilisk venom in your system. We managed – just – to heal you. You need to rest!"

I'd swung myself off the bed, and collapsed immediately. Lau helped me up. "I'm going to *kill* him." I growled.

"Who?" Bianca asked.

"Lupus Helios Soliel Lÿkos. I was not critical!"

"You were." Bianca snapped. I scowled, but then grinned.

"Five shall survive." I grinned.

"How does that make you happy?"

"I guess I'm off the quest now that I'm here. Smeraldo-"

"Who?"

"Guy with the Mark of Mors. He must be the fifth who survived."

Bianca grinned. "That's awesome!" Then she looked at me sternly. "You will be alright in an hour *if you rest for that time*." I pouted, and she sighed. "You can train with us in an hour." I grinned at that, and lay down.

An hour later, I was in the training area fighting Albus.

I didn't hold back.

A few minutes later, I was backed up against the wall, with his sword at my neck. I cursed. "Again." I spat.

"Nope!" Bianca lifted her sword. "My turn!"

"You've been fighting him for ages!" I yelled.

"Ladies."

"Yeah, but he needs to fight and lose."

"*Ladies.*"

"I need practice fighting a more powerful person!"

"Girls!" Stren yelled.

"What!" We yelled at him.

He touched an imaginary wristwatch. "Time."

I glanced at Bianca. "We fight."

"Deal." She grinned. Stren flew out of range.

A few more minutes later, I found myself on my back with Bianca's sword at my neck. I cursed again. "Again." I said.

"Stren's turn."

I pouted but moved away. I sat on a rock, and observed their styles. The problem was, they seemed almost playful when they fought. Finally, I got sick of it. "Guys!" I yelled at them. They turned questioningly. "You seem to be playing, not training. Fight properly."

Bianca grinned. "Shield yourself." I murmured a quick spell. "Done!"

They went again, and I did another spell so that I could track their movements easily. It was...different. They were so fluid, and seemed to be engaged in a deadly dance. They would have chopped each other into pieces if they weren't so quick. They were graceful, and ended the duel as all other similar duels ended. But this was a little different. Bianca pushed him, but held him by the collar of his shirt, with her hair covering both their faces. They exchanged a few words, and Bianca must have blushed, since her neck turned red. They finally relaxed their position, and brushed hands. I hid a smile. It was obvious they liked each other, and they must have made an impromptu decision to get together, like Helios and I had.

My smile fell off. I still hadn't forgiven him. I shoved my hands into my pockets, and froze. There was a bit of paper in one of them. I took it out slowly, and read it. I read it, and smiled sadly. Written on it, in Helios' untidy scrawl, was:

Sorry.

━━━━◈◈◈━━━━

I leaned back, covered in sweat. "How do you do it?" I demanded, once I got my breath back. I'd lost the past four duels, and was both physically and magically exhausted.

Bianca glanced at me, and wordlessly handed me a bottle. "Drink. I'll teach you a couple of spells."

I obediently drank. It was *dýnami*, but with something extra. I got some Magical energy as well. I stood up and turned to Bianca. "Well, Luminis?"

She grinned. I regretted saying that. I had the most tiring training session I had ever had in my life, learning new worded and wordless spells, learnt to summon White Pure form, and withstand powerful attacks on my mind.

At the end of the session, I collapsed. The Seven came up, and I smiled at them, too tired to say a word. "Tired?" Lau asked.

I nodded. "Dead." I said, my throat raw. I pulled myself up with a grimace. "You do this everyday?"

Selena smiled mischievously. "Bia is a *very* demanding tutor."

"Bianca." Aforementioned girl snapped.

"Not Bianca, Elemental." A figure materialized in front of us. Then two. Three. Several figures appeared before us. "Hemera Bianca Ella Elementa Luminis Komistís."

We knelt. The ancients. What were they doing here? One of them turned to Stren. "You shall be Iskios Albus Stren Elementa Patronus Kynigós."

"Be true to your names, Shadow Hunter, Light Bringer." They disappeared.

Immediately, there was a babble of speech. "Was that-"

"The ancients-"

"Why-"

"*Shadow Hunter?*"

Finally, Bianca – or Hemera – yelled, "Shut up!"

Immediately, it ceased. "It seems the Ancients have decided to come visit us, and bless us."

"No, really?" I asked, my voice dripping with sarcasm.

She shot me a look. "Cut it out. Do we announce it to the rest of Camp?"

I shook my head. "It may surprise Malvagita."

"He's an ancient himself."

I shrugged. "Then tell them."

"Sure?"

"Positive."

They stepped towards the Auditorium, when I felt a pull into another dimension. I yelled, but it was soon cut off as I was whisked into another dimension.

You know what happened then, so let's skip that part. When Hemera said, "Time to read", the questers groaned. "C'mon, Hemera!" Karus – Placo – said. "We're tired!"

"Me too." I said. Immediately, Helios was fussing over me. "I was training!"

"Now?!" He yelled.

I rolled my eyes. "I'm fine."

"Really?" He asked, and then shook his head. "Never mind. Hemera wouldn't have let you train otherwise."

I nodded. "Just remind me never to challenge these two to a duel, unless I have been properly tutored, and have gotten a surprise or two up my sleeve."

Helios grinned. He turned to Iskios (I'm gonna call him Albus for the rest of the report. Its less confusing.). "Wanna fight?" He asked.

I face-palmed. "Did you not hear what I said?" I demanded. After what I saw – well, I don't want them going full out on him.

"Worried?" Hemera said teasingly.

"Weren't you when you duel Iskios?"

"Call me Albus," said boy cut in, oblivious to Hemera's blush. "Iskios is…weird."

I pursed my lips, and turned to Helios. "You come back in one piece, okay, Giatró?"

"Yes, Bellator!" He turned to Albus with a small grin. "Ready?"

"When you are." Albus shot back, mirroring Helios' grin. I smiled. This would be interesting.

XXII

Máni

I shook my head at Helios, pursing my lips. "Don't freak out." I murmured to Hemera.

She raised an eyebrow, curious. "What do you mean, Artemis?"

"Call me Máni. Artemis is too formal. And I won't say any more, Hemera."

"Call me Bianca. Tell me."

I smiled a bit. "No can do. However, don't freak out."

She tilted her head, but nodded. "And don't tell Albus anything!" She grinned. "He doesn't need to know. He's gotten better."

"Tell me about it," Antheia grumbled, coming up behind us. "I haven't been able to defeat him even once, I tried so many times. And then it turns out, he was holding back!" She shook her head. "I dunno what Helios was thinking when he challenged him."

I grinned at her. "Worried, are we?" I asked slyly.

She blushed. "No, I'm not! Well, ye- but no- stop laughing!"

"Sorry," I gasped, and then doubled over laughing again. Bianca joined me.

Antheia stamped her foot. "Shut up!" It didn't have the intended effect, as she was still blushing.

"When your finished!" Astrum yelled at us.

I rolled my eyes. "Ready!"

And they began.

It was pretty simple, but they both got bored soon enough. Albus was the first to increase his ferocity, but Helios defended himself with ease. They kept increasing their strength, but neither managed to get an advantage. I don't know about Albus, but Helios was going full out now. Then, he grinned. I groaned.

In three seconds, there was a white wolf with the mark of the Sun on its back standing in the middle of the arena, with its forelegs on Albus chest, and the latter's swords out of reach. Albus grinned. "I yield." Helios got off and transformed. "Cool!" Albus said, his grin widening.

Helios flashed a smile. "Thanks."

"I'm impressed." Antheia said, dusting her hands (She'd been sitting on the ground).

"I'm glad. It's not often that you get impressed." Helios smiled.

She grinned. "Ready to read now?" She asked, tilting her head.

"Uh, no thank you. I'll just go, um, freshen up."

"You look fresh," I said, coming closer.

He shot me a look. "C'mon, Bell." He pleaded.

"Ooh, Bell!" I said, grinning. "Interesting nickname, don't you think, Bianca?"

"Absolutely." It took all my self-control not to burst out laughing again. They both were blushing a bright red.

"Bia?" Albus came up behind us. "We need to start."

I turned to her. "Bia?"

My question was answered as the word left my mouth. "How many times do I tell you not to call me that?"

He shrugged. "I lost count after fifty."

She rolled her eyes and turned to the five of us. "You have five minutes. If you are not here by that time, I will come and get you personally. Clear?"

"Yup." We all said, and went to freshen up.

———❖———

Five minutes later, Helios, Antheia and I were the only ones in the Arena. Five minutes later, Bianca and Albus came up, pulling Astrum and Karus with them.

"Sorry!" Astrum was telling them. "Lost track of time."

"And what exactly were you doing?" Bianca demanded, stopping next to us.

Astrum glared at her. "I was trying to find a way to multiply the lenses and get each of the Seven plus the five of us a pair."

"Oh." She said. "And did you?"

"Yes." He grinned.

"Well?"

He held his hand out. Bianca hesitantly handed the lenses over. He closed his eyes, and waved his hand over it. He murmured something too quick for me to catch, and took a deep breath. He slowly raised his hand from above the lenses, pulling his hands away slowly, with the lenses floating between them. He seemed to be using a lot of energy physically, because he seemed to be actually pulling something, like a super-strong elastic band.

I suddenly realized I hadn't been breathing, and drew a breath as softly as I could. Then I went back to staring at what he had been doing. I gasped.

He had literally *pulled* two pairs of lenses from the original. He repeated the process five times, and then did a slightly modified version of the spell, pulling only one copy from the original. Then, he handed each of them to us, and slouched, exhausted. I handed him my bottle of *Dýnami*, and put the lenses on.

"Whoa." I was stunned.

"What?" Astrum asked.

"Put them on." I said, my eyes wide. I was able to see everything absolutely clearly, even those that were too far for the normal human eye to see. Beyond *infinity.*

"I see what you mean." Astrum said. "Look at it. Its *huge*."

"What are you talking about?" I asked.

"The library?"

"What?" I demanded.

"What do you see?"

"I have much clearer vision, and I can see much further than before. I think I can even shoot that tree over there."

"The one in at the edge of the training ground?" He asked.

"No, further."

"Put yours on, the rest of you." Astrum ordered. "Tell me what you see, one by one."

Helios saw what kind of wolf form people would get. He also saw old wounds, hidden wounds, and poisons in peoples systems. He managed to remove the burns that Malvagita and Cattiva had put on some of our arms (Long story) completely. Well, no one complained.

Antheia saw the enemy. She saw their size, their resources, the – well, you get the idea. I thought she saw something else, but I let it go for the moment. Karus saw the best way to avoid fighting, to keep peace. Bianca and Albus saw the Darkest pockets in the world. The rest of the Seven saw nothing.

"Here's what I think is happening." Astrum said. "Each of us see what-"

"Will help us fulfill what we were meant to do. Máni – the hunter." Antheia continued.

"Karus – the Peace-keeper."

"Bianca – Light Bringer."

"Albus – Shadow hunter."

"Helios – the Healer."

"Antheia – the Warrior."

"Astrum – Wisdom and Knowledge."

"The rest of you haven't been given any official titles yet."

They nodded, and took the scroll from Bianca. Then they turned to Astrum. "I don't suppose there's any way to duplicate this?"

"What's the point?" He asked. Then, he summoned a bunch of scrolls, seemingly from thin air. "Take one, and read."

"One second, Bianca," Antheia interrupted. "I want to try just one more time."

She raised her eyebrows. "Sure?"

"Absolutely." They went to the center of the arena, and started.

Predictably, the duel ended in five minutes. Unbelievably, Antheia won.

"How?" Bianca raised her eyebrows, flabbergasted.

She grinned. "Three words - Bellator, the Warrior."

"You see something else, don't you?" I said, glaring.

She grinned. "I'll show you." She waved her sword.

I grabbed my own, and took my stance. As soon as it began, I felt like I was losing control. Finally, with a combination of a disarming spell and a deft flick of the wrist, she disarmed me. "How?"

"Your weakness is that you're brilliant at doing magic, and at fighting, but not at doing both at the same time. You try fighting with one hand and doing magic with the other. Don't. Channel your magic through your weapon. And by the way, you need a shorter sword. Or maybe a long knife."

I blinked once. Twice. Thrice. "Um, OK."

"And mine?" Bianca cut in.

"You're afraid to hurt you're opponent. That's why you don't go full out. Even against Albus, you didn't go full out. You should focus on developing your magical abilities."

Bianca nodded in a business like way. "Albus?"

Antheia cast a calculating look in his direction. "I don't know. I need to see." She waved her sword, but she didn't seem enthused about it.

Then she started the duel, immediately after he drew his sword. Immediately, the duel went in her direction. Then he snarled, and slashed his sword. A blast of wind blasted her back, but she managed to land on her feet, and hissed. *Little cat...well, maybe not so little.* I thought.

Albus spun his sword in a circle, but before it closed, Antheia threw a ribbon, of all things. Albus sneered, and tried to knock it away with his sword. Predictably, his sword got tangled up, and he lost it. He drew his second, but lost it the second he drew it, when Antheia did some roundabout spell to knock the sword out of his hand. He drew a little dagger. I didn't know what it was, but Helios and Bianca did, and they rushed to stop whatever he was doing.

"Stren, no!" Bianca yelled, grabbing his hand. Helios stepped in front of Antheia, looking every bit as fierce as a werewolf could, which, I tell you, is a lot. Antheia tried to push him away, but Helios growled. Bianca stepped in front of Albus. "Stren, Listen. Calm down. Put it down." She talked to him, and his expression cleared. He blinked, and murmured, "Ells?" Then he looked down, and stiffened. He dropped the knife, and glanced at Bianca. "Ells, I swear, I didn't mean to. I don't know-"

"Its OK. I understand. I'll keep it for now, alright? Relax." She released him, and took hold of the knife.

"What is that thing?" I asked, confused.

"That's the Orcus." I drew a sharp breath. The Orcus – probably the most dangerous weapon in the history of the Elementals.

Legend goes that during an attack, Télos Elementa had told his most skilled smiths to forge a knife so powerful that a single cut would be enough to destroy the enemy. They agreed, but their leader asked for an oath, that the knife would be used only to defend the Elementals of Castra (that is camp). Télos agreed. True to his word, he used it only kill the enemy. But another Elemental, whose identity is unknown, killed Télos and stole the knife. Word is that the Knife was cursed since then. No one knew where it was, or whether is truly was cursed, but there it was.

"The- the Orcus?" Astrum choked out, stunned. "How?"

"I found it in one of the unused sheds." Albus said in a shaky voice. "God, Antheia, I'm so sorry. I was so stupid…"

She gave a tentative smile. "I guess it really is cursed."

"How do you know?" Helios asked.

"I'm Bellator." She walked to Bianca unsteadily, and reached out hesitantly. "I'll try to remove it."

Bianca nodded, and gave her the weapon, sheathed.

"Wish me luck." She said, taking a deep breath.

XXIII

Antheia

I tilted the sheathed weapon, and then pulled it out. I couldn't help myself. I gasped.

It was the most beautiful weapon ever made, pitch black with silver designs, made with precision to say two words – De Orcus. The hit and cross-guards were also black, but they had white in them as well. There was a single Opal in the middle of one of the cross-guards. But that wasn't why I gasped.

The curse in the knife was very powerful. It was too powerful for the knife, which led me to think that either the curse got more powerful with time, which I found unlikely, or others had tried to remove the curse, and the energy had been absorbed by the existing curse.

I tilted the blade in my hand, careful not to let it draw a single drop of blood in my hand. There were more words written on the knife, and I scowled. "Helios – Paper, pen. Note down what I say - Ut supra maledictio, exagníseis me, Hemera Komistís, Iskios Kynigós, Bellator Proelia."

I frowned. It seemed too simple. Bianca started saying, "Kath-"

"Wait!" I yelled, sheathing the blade.

"What?" She asked, frowning.

"The curse- it adds the strength of other spells to its own."

99

"How do you know that?" Bianca demanded.

I shared my memories with her. Not as simple as it may seem, but it can be done. She nodded, and stepped forward. Albus came as well, their own (thankfully normal) knives in hand. I drew my own, and knelt, placing the knife in the ground in front of me. The other knelt opposite me. "Who's first?" I asked, nervous.

"Me." Bianca said quietly. She held her wrist above the Orcus, and brought her knife down, making a cut on her wrist. Three drops of blood dripped onto the hilt of the Orcus, shining like little red stars in the black sky. Bianca drew her hand back a bit, but she grit her teeth, and let another drop fall. And another. And another. When the seventh drop fell, she drew her hand back, but didn't heal it, pressing the wound onto her dress. She nodded tersely to Albus. He grabbed his knife and made another cut. This time he let the drops fall on the qillion. At the sixth drop he twitched his hand, and a drop nearly fell on the blade. My hand shot towards his, and I caught it. *How did I do that?* I wondered. Then it was my turn. I took the knife, and made a small cut on my wrist. The red drops fell onto the blade one by one.

One. The red looked startling against the black of the knife.

Two. I could see the curse flowing into the droplets.

Three. It flowed into my body. For a moment, I felt like grabbing the knife and killing everybody in the vicinity.

Four. Pain. Impossible pain, flowing through my blood vessels to my heart.

Five. It has reached my heart. I tried to force it out, but it got stronger.

Six. I wanted to just crawl into fetal position, till I die.

Seven. The pain was receding, and I pulled my hand away from the blade.

It was still there, but I managed to rasp, "It needs three more on the sheath."

"One from each?" I was surprised by how weak Albus' voice sounded.

I shook my head. "Blood merge?" Bianca said, her voice shaking. I nodded.

She pulled out the sheath, and held out her wrist. I held out mine, and held our cuts together. Albus hesitated, and joined us. Our combined blood fell onto the sheath, three lone drops.

Your Name, Bianca. I told her through MindSpeech.

"Sum, Hemera Bianca Ella Elementa Luminis Komistís, Katharíste hac telo!" I cleanse this blade. Her voice seemed to echo, creating a sort of hum around us.

"Sum, Iskios Albus Stren Elementa Patronus Kynigós, hac telo!" His voice added to the hum, and I realized there was a sort of shield around us.

"Sum," I started, and the pain increased. "Bellator Antheia Jeune Proelia," I bit out. "Katharíste hac telo!" I screamed the last part out, the hum becoming louder and louder with every word.

The blade glowed, and I collapsed.

Simultaneously, I think I heard two other thuds next to me, but I wasn't too sure.

XXIV

Helios

"That was a stupid, foolish thing to do, Helios."

"Okay! Give me a break, Karus! I got worried!"

I was seriously getting tired of talking about it. As soon as Antheia collapsed, I had run straight to her. The good news – the shield around the three of them had collapsed as soon as they did. The bad news – a blast of energy had shot out, almost knocking me out as well. Fortunately, Karus erected a shield in front of me. And now, he was chewing me out.

"That's not-"

A loud thud interrupted him. We turned to Bianca, trying not to grin. She had, literally, gotten out of the wrong side of the bed. We'd kept their swords over there, and she'd fallen right on them. I helped her up, and gave her swords back to her. "The other two?" she asked.

"They're fine." I told her, grinning. "We didn't expect you to wake up first."

"That's why you kept these over here, I suppose." She gestured towards the weapons and glared.

"Vigilaveris!" We heard a sharp voice say from the bed on Bianca's right. Antheia was getting up.

"Antheia!" I said, frowning. "You need to rest!"

She, naturally, ignored me. "There's one more thing we need to do."

"What?" Albus asked, having been woken up by Antheia.

"Name the Knife's Master." She was met by a confused silence. "Honestly?" She sighed. "A weapon's master is the only one who can use it. He or she can control the weapon to a large extent. Mostly a weapon's master is the maker. But sometimes, the master is to be named, like when there is more than one maker, or the weapon's original master has died. That's the case here." She turned to Bianca and Albus. "It needs to be one of the three of us, since we used our blood."

"It needs to be someone who can control himself or herself." Bianca said.

"It needs to be someone who knows about weapons." Albus added.

"You." They both said together.

"M-Me?" Antheia stuttered. "But you are the leaders!"

"I lost control while fighting you." Albus said.

"I am too controlled. You said it yourself. I need to fight more confidently before I gain mastery of such a dangerous weapon."

Antheia bit he lip, and I moved forward. "Do it, Antheia."

She turned to me and looked me in the eye. *Are you sure?* She asked me silently with her eyes. I nodded. She took a deep breath, and took the knife. "De Orcus, emeís Ónoma domini tui." We name your master.

"Aftí Apoteleí Herba, Natus." Bianca knelt near Antheia's bed. She is the plant, the Warrior.

"Aftí Apoteleí Bellator Proelia." Albus knelt on the other side of the bed.

"Ego Sum Bellator Antheia Jeune Proelia." I am Bellator Antheia Jeune Proelia.

Antheia blinked. "It will not hurt me." She said, staring at the knife. She got off the bed, and pulled Bianca and Albus up. "I'm going to make a belt for this thing," she told me. "Wanna come and help?"

"No, you will not make a belt now. Yes, I will help you later." I glared at her.

"Will too!" She grinned cheekily at me. "I'm all better!"

"That," I said, striding across, "is for me to decide. I *am* Giatró."

I did a full checkup, and it turned out she was fully recovered. I still went with her, making sure she didn't exert herself.

Four hours later, we walked out of the armory with a silver belt at Antheia's waist, De Orcus (Which I was still very wary of) in its sheath, her sword in another, her spear strapped to her back, a shield on her arm, and her helmet under her other. She was wearing Greek-style armor (Silvery, with just a light tinge of green), and seemed rather confident. I told her so, and she replied, "I don't feel it."

I grinned at her. "You'd best take that armor off, Ant, if you don't want Bianca to kill you by making you read with that on."

She rolled her eyes, but went and changed into jeans and a purple T-shirt. "C'mon, G."

That night, we had the best night's sleep in what seemed like ages, but we didn't sleep for long. Bianca decided it was time to get everyone to learn as much as they could without exhausting themselves, since the attack had been postponed by a day. All the Elementals – including the Egyptians, some Spaniards, three Greeks, and two Italians who kept arguing with the Greeks – had come to Camp.

"We'll decide a proper system to get Elementals in other countries, but lets focus on this now. Plants – focus on creating illusions – it'll confuse them. Arbre – join the Flower Elementals – no complaints – and help them with their fighting. Isabella – get those five to work together." She gestured towards the Greeks and Italians. She continued in this manner, making sure everyone focused on what they were weakest at.

Once everyone started, Bianca and the rest of the Seven walked around and helped everyone improve. Then Pas and Estre came, and helped Albus and Bianca train respectively. The rest of the Seven went to a corner and did their training together. Antheia, at one point, went and told each person to work on his or her weakness, and we could see that everybody listened.

After another two hours, we took a break. Everyone was dead tired, and the Spaniards, Abril, Adella, Eloy, and Augusto, collapsed on the floor of the training arena. Bianca went and gave them water, made them stand, and sent them to eat.

We had some time to relax, and I decided it would be perfect to test something I'd wanted to test for some time. I closed my eyes, and thought, *Smeraldo?*

About time. He said. I groaned. I really didn't want an Elemental-turned-wolf-turned-immortal in my head, but I didn't see any choice.

Too right, Lupus.

Oh, shut up.

Now is that any way to talk to an immortal?

I groaned again. This was going to be a long day.

XXV

Karus

After the training session, Bianca gave us time to get acquainted, and become friendly. She glared at the Greeks and the Italians, who meekly got up and walked away from each other. I think the Italians are from Rome, which must be why they argue so much. One of the Greeks, Alexis, who told me to call him Alex, was a stone Elemental.

"What's your specialty?"

"Topaz, but I can do other stones as well. You?"

"Sapphire, but I can do blue topaz as well. That's the only other stone I can do."

I glanced at him. "You and I'll work on that when we begin again. For now, let's eat." He muttered something about us working too hard. I turned to him. "It's a war. What did you expect? Stay in bed till noon, and no training?"

"Is that how you were? I can't imagine you having many threats." Then he paused. "No offense."

"No, of course not." I muttered sarcastically. "No, we like to keep on our toes," I said aloud. "We have war games now and then, but we haven't for a while."

"War games?" Alex asked, his eyes wide. "Cool!"

"If you have an Elementa, preferably Bianca, on your side. Of course, Albus is OK too, but we prefer having Bianca."

"Nice to see I'm so loved, Karus."

I grinned at Juliet. "You've been keeping a low profile, Jules."

She had me pinned to the ground in two seconds flat. "Don't. Call. Me. Jules."

"Two seconds, Elementa. You're losing touch."

"I can still beat you in three seconds in the Arena."

I raised my eyebrows. "Wanna bet, *Jules*?"

I flipped and sent her to the ground and had her pinned to the wall next to me in five seconds.

There was a cough next to us. "You guys are too violent."

"Aw, is the Graeca getting soft?"

Alex growled at the Italian. "We'll see who's getting soft, you little-"

"What did I tell you, Ells? *It's impossible.*" Isabella and Bianca came next to us.

Bianca raised her eyebrows at Juliet, and in three seconds, I was on the ground (again) with my dagger at my throat. I grinned and said, "Let's deal with these two, and then we can continue this later." I turned to them, and grinned. "I am Placo Eiríni. You guys play nice, or I'll make you."

"Shut up!" The Greek and Italian said simultaneously.

Ten minutes later, they both had agreed on a truce until the final battle (as the war came to be dubbed – stupid, if you ask me) got over. I had to show them a few visions about what would happen if peace was not kept. I had to show the Aurora as well. Finally, they decided to play nice. I turned to Juliet and pretended to wipe my brow. "Phew!" I said, and then grinned. "Hungry?" I asked the group. The girls groaned and face-palmed.

After eating, I decided to gather my fellow Stone Elementals, and help them increase their scope. Everyone tried to keep each other's spirits high (Even the Greeks and Romans!), but everyone was feeling tenser by the minute. *Today's the day*, I thought, going for a bit of practice with the Seven. The other four and Juliet were also there. I nodded to them, and we got to it. Antheia told me that my weakness was once I suffered a setback, even a minor one, I froze momentarily. I worked on that, and she said I was much better.

After another two-and-a-half hours, we decided to take another break. I walked to Juliet and told her, "We need to shift this to somewhere near the Charging area. Or get the Elementals to make their own personal mini charger."

"Option B." She replied distractedly.

"Jules, what's wrong?" I asked.

She smiled. "Nothing. What makes you think that something's wrong?"

"You're tensed up. You're gripping your hilt hard. You're jumpy. I've only seen you this tense when you challenged Cattiva-" My eyes widened. "Oh, God. That's it, isn't it?"

She nodded. "I can't help but feel that I'm missing something. Some vital detail…" She trailed off, and then sighed in frustration. "It's there, but I can't tell what it is." She thought about it.

"Well, maybe-" I started.

"God, that's it!" She raced off, told Bianca something, and left the area. I blinked, and then shrugged.

I walked to Bianca. "Time?" I asked. She nodded.

We had gotten everybody to make their own personal mini charger, and got each of them to charm it so that only he or she could get the magic from his or her charger. They were currently installing it onto a place in their armor. I walked up to them.

"Ok, everybody," I yelled, lifting my own. "Suit up!"

They started wearing their armor. I was already wearing mine, so I just had to wear my belt and make sure everything was in place. I walked around and helped everyone get in the armor. "Ready?" I yelled, once I was finished. "Yeah!" They shouted enthusiastically.

"Not at all." Someone murmured next to me. I turned and saw Máni. "You?"

"I'll be OK." I smiled, and helped her tighten her belt. "You'll be great."

She grinned. "You too, Placo." She went to her battle group, the Weres. I turned to mine, the Sedja. I lifted my spear, signaling for them to fall in in their ranks. Everybody quieted down, and fell in. I signaled for them to move forward. We stood in front of Bianca, Albus, and Juliet. I nodded to them, and they nodded back.

Once everybody had assembled, Bianca raised her had for silence. In two seconds, the only sound was that of the breeze outside. *Ten minutes.*

"Many of you have fought the Dark before," she began. "You know that it is manipulative, and brings out the darkest part of you." She turned her head to look at everyone. "But you know that we can fight. We can stop the Darkness, and protect the balance." She raised her head ever so slightly, and grinned fiercely. "Each and every one of us, no matter what little power we have, can fight. Together, we will set the balance right." She raised her voice. "Together, we shall win!" She raised her spear, and everybody cheered. "March!" She ordered, and each group went to their position.

At the head of the Sedja, I thought, *Nine minutes.*

XXVI

Astrum

Stella Estrella (The Stars Elementals' leader) and I led the rest of the Astraeus, our battle group, into position. We were on the North Petal, and I was standing on Stella's left. "Stella, Spear." I reminded her, and she nodded. She drew her spear out, and held it ready. "Charge it." She started, and smiled at me sheepishly. She charged it, and put a finger to her lips. Then she tapped her left wrist. I made a fist and stuck my thumb out, telling her six minutes until show time. Then we looked forward, and making sure I had a good view. On an impulse, I wore the lenses (I'd charmed them so that they were lenses – corrective lenses with power 0). I had a feeling I'd need them in the battle.

Astrum? Stella asked me through her communication stone.

Yeah?

Is that armor the Estrella *armor?*

I was silent for a moment. Then I said, *Yes.*

The *Estrella* armor is the armor that is given to a third generation Star Elemental. Elementals very rarely have the same Elemental powers across generations. I was the fourth generation Stars Elemental, and hence I inherited the armor. If I had been of any other Element, I wouldn't have received the armor. The armor was silvery, and enchanted to be as light as – well – starlight. It was not very inconspicuous, but it was strong, and believe me, in this battle, I needed strong.

Ten. I thought.

Nine.

Eight.

Seven.

Six.

Five. I lifted my spear, and signaled to the rest of the Astraeus group.

Four.

Three.

Two. I stood in defense position.

One.

And all hell broke loose.

The Skiá just kept coming. Fortunately for us, they were easy to destroy. I slashed my sword (the spear seemed impractical, so I'd decided to use the sword) and got three Skiá at one shot. They dissolved into black smoke. Four more came at me, and I got them as well. Then – well, you get the idea.

"Regroup!" I yelled, seeing that we'd been too scattered. Fortunately, we'd thought to charm ourselves so that our voices would reach all those whom we wanted to hear us. Then, Bianca sent me a MindMessage. *Come to the center. Now.*

I went to the center, just as the Seven and the other four came to me.

"Placo, what do you think of this message?" Bianca showed him a grey piece of paper. He paled, and then took his set of lenses from his pocket. He scanned it for a moment, and glanced up. "Genuine." Bianca's eyes narrowed. "Impossible." She muttered.

They shared memories, and Bianca became nervous. "What do I do?" She moaned. "This is crazy!"

"What is?" I asked.

"This." She handed the paper to me. I read it, and took a step back. "No, no, no, no. This is not happening."

"Astrum?" Antheia asked. "What's going on?"

I showed her the paper, and she dropped it like she'd been stung.

"What now?" She asked.

"Now, we call a meeting."

XXVII

Karus

Bianca called the leaders of the Elementals and the leaders of the other branches of Elementals. As soon as they'd all come, she held out her hand, and said, "Ruhe." Every single one of us glared at her. "It's necessary." She snapped, unrepentant. "I don't want anyone yelling and screaming after I say the first sentence."

The leaders rolled their eyes, but the Seven, Juliet, and the five of us maintained grim expressions. *And the rest of us?* I asked her through the stone.

She glanced at us, and said, "Sie können sprechen."

"We got a problem." Antheia said, pursing her lips. "A *big* problem."

"We got a letter," Bianca started. Every rolled their eyes, except for the thirteen of us. "From Malvagita Ubella." Everybody's jaw dropped.

"It said," Albus continued, "and I quote, 'Can we meet at sunrise? There are a few important things we need to discuss. I'd call a temporary truce, but the Skiá are out of my control. I'll explain everything when we meet. Malvagita.'"

Lúmine raised her hand, and Bianca removed the spell. "How do you know it's genuine?"

"Karus is Placo. He ought to know, even if the rest of us don't." Albus replied. Lúmine nodded. Everyone looked at me.

"It's definitely genuine. Also," I hesitated, then ploughed forward. "Several things about this don't add up. This isn't his, of lack of a better word, style. Consilium?" I turned to Astrum.

He nodded. "He may be – no, he is – Dark, but not completely. He would *not* attack Camp with such numbers. They tend to be... subtler. This outright attack... it seems wrong."

"Even during the quest," Antheia said, "the protections? They were one hundred percent dark, which is *definitely* not his style. He usually has a bit of light in each and every one of his spells." The other twelve nodded. "Even during your double duel," she turned to Bianca and Albus.

"They didn't use completely dark spells." Selena said. "After the war, I read up on what he'd done, that 'experiment', and I found that that's actually an ancient way of sharing Elemental power. We'd assumed that it was the 'chargers' that recharged the leaders' amulets, but it seemed that the stone is a 'collector'."

"Elemental energy from each of the Elementals flowed from fourteen Elementals – Earth, Air, Fire, Water, Sun, Moon, Gems, Rainbow, Animals, Plants, Flowers, Stars, White Elemental, and Dark Elemental – to the 'collector'. The magic was then distributed evenly between the 14 Elementals, with the Dark and White Elementas getting the maximum energy." Lau looked at all of us, seeing if we got it.

Pianta took over the explanation from Lau. "Malvagita modified it so that he was the only one who got the energy. Since he was more powerful than all of them, he had a perfect balance of energy. He used only dark magic, to keep up appearance, so to speak, but at his headquarters, he used only balanced spells, occasionally even White spells. He never did any of this in front of the 13 other Elementals involved in the spell."

There was a stunned silence. "So you're telling me," Lúmine said, "that Malvagita is actually a balanced Elemental." She stated.

Cielo nodded. "We don't know about now, but earlier, he was balanced."

"Then why did he use the leaders?"

"My guess," Stervia said, "is that they wanted to throw us off track."

"The question now," Cielo said, "is who goes to meet them. We know Bianca and Albus have to go, but who else goes?"

One of the Greeks, Alexis, if I remember rightly, raised his hand. Bianca removed his silence. "I think you thirteen should go." He stated.

The Italian raised his hand. Bianca let him speak, but not before telling him, "Don't fight." He grinned, and then said, "Lúmine as well." He grinned. "She is, if I'm not mistaken, the only other Elementa here."

Stervia nodded. "One more person."

"Alexis." The Italian stated. Everyone stared at him. "What? He's the best person to go. Then you'll have 3 stone Elementals." He glared at Alexis. "Don't let it go to your head, but you are the only one powerful enough to go."

Alexis blinked. "Thanks, man." He clapped the other guy's shoulder. "You're not so bad."

"You know something?" The Italian asked. "You're not so bad yourself."

XXVIII

Máni

"Where are we going to meet him anyway?" I asked Bianca.

"The letter will take us there." She said shortly.

"The le- oh." I nodded. "Transportation spell." *How many things can we use for transportation? The wall, the potion, the spell – and that's just three of them!*

"Are we going as Eirineftí, or as Agonistón?" Astrum asked Bianca.

"*What!*" She asked, confused. I glanced at him ant tilted my head, confused as well.

Astrum sighed. "Peacefully, or as warriors?"

"Warriors."

Astrum nodded, and then told all of us to gather round in a circle. He then drew a few strange symbols on the ground in front of each and every one of us. Mine was the Prima Lingua rune for A.

"What's this?" Albus asked, the same moment Bianca said, "You're joking."

"Take your spears, everybody," Astrum said, ignoring both of them.

"I don't have one," Lúmine and Alexis said at the same time.

Astrum rolled his eyes and snapped, "Káno." Make. Two spears materialized in front of them. "They're already charged." He went to his own spot. "Touch the symbol in front of you with the head." We did that, and waited. *Say Eínai.* He told us through the stone (We'd given it to the other Elementals earlier.). "Eínai." Be. I felt a rush of power, and I blinked. A silvery mist gathered around me, and dissipated almost as quickly. I blinked again, and looked up. Everybody else looked up at the same moment. They seemed as shocked as I was.

"What," I said, glaring at Astrum, "exactly, was that?"

"You are who you are." He said calmly.

I stared at him. "What are you *wearing*?" I demanded, shocked. He was wearing a *cape.* I stared at it. He *hates* capes. Unless something changed in the past two minutes, other than our clothes, he still hates capes.

"A cape." He pursed his lips. Good. Still hates capes.

Then I looked at the others.

Bianca wore her armor, with swords and spear, which had turned into Lámpsi ánthi (Metal - Long story). She was also wearing a helmet, which had a white horse plume. Albus was wearing the same thing. Neither had capes, but they had a Lutetium circlet/crown thing, signifying leadership of the non-ancient Elementals. Karus was wearing a tunic, pants, and his sword and spear. Helios was dressed similarly, but he had a canteen (of healing potion, probably) in his belt. He also had a – was that a first aid kit? I blinked. Antheia was wearing armor, but she had a few extra knives – in her boots, her belt, her arm (the kind that'll come to your hand if you flicked your wrist), and that was not counting de Orcus. As for me…

I looked down and blinked again. *What was I wearing!*

Astrum stifled a laugh. "Dressed for hunting." He said, not quite succeeding. And so I was. I was wearing boots, a white t-shirt, jeans, and a jacket. I had a quiver of arrows on my back, and an extra quiver at my waist. I also had my sword and spear, both of which had turned silver. In fact, everything I was wearing was silvery. "Well," Astrum said, "you *are* a Mond."

The others were wearing armor, and had their swords, shields, helmets, and spears. "Dressed for fulfilling our duties," Bianca said. "Those of us who don't have titles have only their armor and weapons."

I nodded. That made sense, but that didn't mean I had to like it. "Ready to roll?" I asked eyebrows raised.

Bianca nodded. "Usual positions?" She asked. The rest of us (except Lúmine and Alexis) nodded. We stood like an arrowhead, with Bianca at the tip, Albus at her left, Juliet at her right, Pianta and Cielo behind them, followed by Selena and Lau. Behind them were Stervia and Lúmine, Helios and Antheia, Máni and Astrum, and finally Karus and Alexis.

"Ready?" Bianca asked. The rest of us answered affirmative. She activated the spell, and we were off.

XXIX

Helios

We left Camp, hoping that the spell will be slow. But, all too soon, we had reached. Malvagita and Cattiva were waiting. But there was something different about them.

"What's wrong with your eyes?" Bianca – no, Hemera, I reminded myself – asked. Their eyes were brown rather than black – a soft, almost chocolate brown.

Malvagita sighed. "This was how we were before."

"Before what?" Selena asked.

Hemera answered. "The betrayal. *His* betrayal."

"I didn't mean to, Elena." Malvagita said, eyes sad.

"You did anyway." Hemera said. I assumed she was translating what Estre said.

"No! I didn't!" He exclaimed. "Well, I did, but I didn't. Not really."

"Thanks." Hemera said, her voice dripping with sarcasm. "That really clears things up."

Malvagita bit his lip, and then pulled up his sleeve. On it was a small black burn. I didn't recognize it, but evidently, Hemera and Iskios did. "How-"

"When-"

"What-"

"Why-"

"Who?"

"I'll answer the last question first, shall I?" Malvagita asked, amused. Hemera nodded sharply, gripping her sword's hilt with one hand. "De Kakós Psychí. The evil soul, the embodiment of evil, the one who makes all black. In all ways, the antithesis of Der Estre Magier."

There was a pause. "So you're saying," said Hemera, breaking the silence, "that everything that you've done, since the beginning of Magic, was actually done by Kakós Psychí?"

"Yes and no. It happened just after our first argument, Elena, when Pas came to camp."

"Wasn't much of a camp, was it?" Hemera said dryly. "There were what, five Elementals, six, if you count Pas?"

"Yeah. Then there were five again, and then there was a drastic increase after," here his face darkened, "after I left." He sighed.

"Before camp, I was always the different one – my Magic kept me apart from everyone else. At first, in camp, I was accepted, but when more White Elementals came, I realized that I was different again – the only dark Elemental. I was slowly pushed away. When Pas came, I wasn't even told – you four just went ahead and found his power. I grew bitter, and that's how Kakós Psychí found me." He smiled wryly. "He whispered sweet promises in my ears, and slowly drew me in. They were all lies." He whispered. "By the time I had realized my mistake, it was too late. He had full control, and I had to leave. I did, but not before Kakós tried to kill you. I realized I needed to leave. I was dangerous, out of my own control." He shook his head. "I still don't know if I did the right thing. In camp, our magic kept him at bay. Once I left, he took full possession of me. That's how I'm still alive. I didn't take an apprentice until Cattiva."

Juliet turned to Cattiva. "And you?" She asked. "Why did you betray camp?"

Cattiva smiled wryly. "I was fading. I'd gotten the Dark amulet, but I charmed everyone to think I'd gotten a White amulet, because of the prejudice against us. I did only White magic, but my magic was receding. A sliver of Kakós came to me, and taught me my magic. I owed him, so I joined him." He shook his head. "Worst decision ever. Enough said."

"Why did you call us?"

Cattiva and Malvagita shared a look. Malvagita took a deep breath. "To destroy him."

We all stiffened. A chill had settled in the room. A soft chuckle echoed in the room. "Naughty, Naughty." All the shadows gathered in front of Hemera. "Hasn't your mother taught you not to needlessly destroy?"

"Hasn't yours?" Malvagita shot back.

The shadows dissipated. In its place stood a young man. He wore a black, long sleeved robe with blood red runes on the bottom. Upon closer inspection, I realized that they spelt out the words 'Kakós Psychí', 'Darkness', and things like that. I stopped reading them, knowing that if I looked at them for too long, I'd be drawn in.

Kakós extended a hand. Immediately, Malvagita collapsed. He grit his teeth, and closed his eyes. Kakós let his hand fall to his side. Malvagita stayed down. Kakós turned, and smiled. "Welcome." His voice sent shivers down my spine. It sounded cold as ice, and yet hot as fire. It sounded dangerous. His eyes were blood red, and his grin was feral. "Welcome to my new home."

"Thank you, Kakós Psychí." If Kakós' voice was cold as ice and hot as fire, Hemera's voice was smooth as water and rough as earth. "It is a pleasure."

"Perhaps you would like to sit?" Kakós tilted his head.

"I'd rather stand, if it's all the same." Hemera's face was a carefully blank mask. "Shall we begin, then?"

Kakós chuckled. "So eager to be destroyed." His face became abruptly serious. "You could be great, you know. All you need to do is join me. You'd be known forever."

"I'd rather be forgotten than be infamous." Hemera raised her chin.

Kakós' smile widened. "So be it."

He raised his hand, and a ball of Darkness gathered in his hand. He hurled it towards Hemera, who summoned a Shield of Light to counter it. The shield expanded, and the Darkness scattered. When the last of the shadows dissipated, we drew our spears. I glanced around, and raised my fist. Hemera nodded. We stood in pairs, back to back, in a rough circle. Hemera stood in the center of the circle, looking for overhead attacks. What happened next, however was completely unexpected.

The ground beneath us erupted, and we fell. Immediately, shadows surrounded us, and I felt the others slip out of reach. I tried struggling, but the Darkness only drew closer.

No! I thought. *I will not give up!* Images flashed before my mind's eye, unbidden. *Karus. Máni. Astrum. Bianca. Albus. God help me – Malvagita and Cattiva. Selena. Lau. Stervia. Pianta. Cielo. Juliet. Antheia.* I froze. *Oh, god. Antheia!* I struggled harder, reaching out with my mind, searching desperately. *Antheia!* I thought of her smile, her laugh, her magic, the time she told me she loved me – I concentrated on that feeling, and reached further.

And the bonds shattered.

The shadows blew apart, seemingly away from me and...

"Antheia."

"Helios." She nodded. We turned to Kakós.

"Impressive." He leaned back on the wall. Antheia and I stood shoulder to shoulder. "Very impressive. Such a waste of talent."

I glared. "Fighting for those whom we love isn't a waste. It's one of the few best things magic can be used for. Magic used with love is more powerful than any other kind of magic."

Kakós smiled. "We'll see."

XXX

Astrum

I glanced at Antheia and Helios. They stood shoulder to shoulder, radiating love and confidence. I glanced at my partner, Máni. We fell in next to the Antheia and Helios. The others joined us, and we raised our spears as one, ready to bravely face our enemy-

Who wasn't there.

"What!"

"Where's he gone?"

"Impossible!"

"Unbelievable!"

Well, you get the idea. I spun around, and muttered a quick reveal spell. As I had expected, nothing came up. I frown and tried to remember a spell to find a Dark soul, but I came up with nothing. I glanced at Máni. She tilted her head to the left. I nodded and turned to the left. Then I spun around and stabbed.

Score. I grinned.

Kakós materialized in front of me, and smiled. Too late, I realized my mistake. He flicked his hand, and I went flying back. "No more holding back!" He laughed, and everything went black.

‑‑‑ ❈ ‑‑‑

When I woke up, there was, predictably, complete chaos. Unexpectedly, Kakós was nowhere to be seen. I cursed, and looked for Máni. She saw me, and came up to me. "I know where he is, but I'm having a hard time communicating. I couldn't feel anybody. It's like having bad signal."

I glanced around. "Even the stone?" I asked.

She nodded. "It's a good thing we practiced those signals. We'd be dead by now if it weren't for them."

Further conversation was interrupted by a loud blast coming from the middle of the room. I spun around again, and stumbled. Malvagita had his black spear out, and was holding Kakós away from Hemera. Kakos growled.

"Don't be a fool, Malvagita," he spat out. "Don't betray the Dark."

Malvagita remained silent for a moment, and then looked Kakós in the eye. "I'm not betraying the dark, I'm righting a wrong."

Kakós sneered. "Do you really believe that the Light will accept you? They rejected you, betrayed you, broke you. You are dark – you are mine!"

Malvagita glared. "I belong to no one. As for me being Dark, without Light, there is no Dark. And without Dark, there is no Light. I may be dark, but I am not evil. It is not the kind of magic a person uses that makes a person evil, it is the way they use it. I am Dark, and they are Light. And together, we will defeat you!"

He pushed Kakós back, and it seemed for a moment, that Kakós was weakening. As soon as the illusion came, however, it was gone. Kakós flicked Malvagita aside like he was nothing more than dirt beneath his shoes. For a moment, Malvagita's eyes met mine. I looked into his eyes, and understood what we needed.

I looked at Máni, and she nodded. "I trust you." No more words were needed. We reached out to each other, and merged.

It was like nothing I'd ever felt before. I felt my senses expand, my eyesight was sharper, I was able to sense everything. *Is this how you feel all the time?* I asked Máni.

Yes.

We hadn't merged just our minds. We were one – mind, body, power. We turned to Kakós, who'd started making his way to us, eyes narrowed. "Impossible!" He gasped, raising his spear. We raised our arm and flicked our wrist. The spear shot out of his hand, and he hissed as though burned.

"Is nothing." We completed his statement. Yes, clichéd, but more than appropriate.

We felt more power add on. *Bring it on!* Alexis mentally yelled. One by one, the Elementals joined the Merge. However, when there were only four Elementals left – Juliet, Hemera, Malvagita and Cattiva – Kakós struck. He leapt towards Juliet, his sword arm brought back to strike –

And was intercepted by Cattiva.

"NO!" I never thought Juliet was capable of making such a sound. We watched, horrified, as she attacked Kakós. Malvagita went to Cattiva, trying to heal him. Hemera hung back, unable to do anything for fear of hurting Juliet.

"Retreat, Juliet!" She yelled, throwing a ball of fire at Kakós. He deflected it easily, but left his right side open. Juliet struck, driving her weapon into his side. Kakós growled, pulled his hand back, and stabbed.

"JULIET!" Hemera screamed, throwing a ball of the four Elements at Kakós, beginning to rush forward. Malvagita grabbed her arm, and shook his head. She hesitated, and then nodded. With one last glare at Kakós, they joined the Merge.

We felt their sorrow and anger at the deaths of Cattiva and Juliet. We felt their need for revenge as our own, and raised our arm. A spear materialized in our palm, and we stabbed at Kakós. He deflected the strike, and returned a strike of his own. We dodged it, and fought back with vigor. The fight was, however, going his way.

Someone needs to take control, Malvagita said.

Who should? Stervia asked.

Malvagita hesitated, and then said, *Hemera.* We felt his sadness at not being able to take revenge personally, and his anger at Kakós.

No, Hemera said. *You and I, Malvagita. Light and Dark. Together. Grey.*

We felt grim satisfaction, and trust. *I trust you,* they said together. The rest of us stopped pushing, and Malvagita and Hemera took control.

If what we had before was complete understanding, then what we had after was a sense of belonging and unity. We couldn't figure out who felt what, but we fought with perfect coordination, as though we were one person. And we were, in a way. We had the experience of the ancients, the senses of the hunter and the Wolves, the restraint of the Healer and peace keeper, the fire of the warrior – what one had, we all had.

Each move was executed perfectly. We covered for our own weaknesses, if that makes sense. We were not different, we were not the same; we were who we were.

Finally, after fighting for an hour – or was it only a few minutes? – we stood in front of Kakós, spear raised. "You were right, Kakós Psychí. No more holding back." Together, we struck, ending the fight, and the existence of Kakós Psychí.

Epilogue

Antheia

I suppose that the others felt that since I started the story, it was only fair that I finished it. Well, a lot happened after the fight.

We got back to camp and honored the two dead: Juliet and Cattiva. They gave their lives for camp, and the 'betrayal' was forgotten.

Camp was rebuilt to be able to include Elementals from different countries. We built new camps where there were more than seven Elementals, which was surprisingly few. Those who wished to remain in camp were free to do so, and many did.

Most importantly, the peace declaration was signed. Dark magic was no longer considered evil, just different. That conception, however, changed soon. Dark magic was just what Light magic was – Magic. There was another cabin for Dark Elementals, which soon expanded as many more people were discovered to have an affinity with Dark magic. Bianca, Albus and Malvagita grew closer, and soon became proficient practitioners of Grey magic.

Those of us who were left of the fifteen, along with Malvagita, became famous amongst the Elementals, and, fortunately or unfortunately, our story became legend.

Magic entered a new age where every thing flourished, and, no kidding, grass grew greener. Elementals grew more powerful, and the legend of the Fifteen (as the war soon came to be called) was soon written in books and kept in the library.

Nothing else changed much, however. The boys still goof around, Albus is still a bit slow, I still keep Helios from getting a big head – we all just have fun.

Elemental Magic is in a new era, and it's time for you to join in. What are you waiting for?

The End

About the Author

Sharada M Subrahmanyam lives among her books. Inspired by the books that she has read by her favourite authors, like Tamora Pierce, Rick Riordan, Christopher Paolini, and Allison Croggon, she wanted to create a world of her own. Her first novel, The Elementals: The Beginning and the End, is an ambitious foray into the world of novel writing. With her second book, she hopes to continue her journey.

She lives in Chennai with her parents. She argues that societies that has a place for stories will be occupied so much that there will be no place for terror. She loves to read and listen to music. Logic fascinates her and she is interested in the workings of the human mind.

She has off late developed a fascination for patterns and opinion formation on the net. She wants to study and work to take advantage of technology to create opinion to change the world.